SAM HAIN
OCCULT DETECTIVE

THE REGENTS

BRON JAMES

SAM HAIN
THE REGENTS

Prologue

He knew they were following him. They had been ever since he'd left the café. He'd seen them there not half an hour ago, sitting only a few tables away from him. Not that he had really paid much attention to them at the time, they had just been on the peripheries of his vision, but now that he was aware they were following him, he couldn't help but notice there was something strange about them.

It wasn't much past ten o'clock when Sam Hain had walked into the café. He had ordered a large cup of tea (English Breakfast, dash of milk), paid for it with a fistful of coins, and sat down at his usual table by the window, looking out onto Hampstead high street. He'd idly watched people wander back and forth past the window, going about their day, and he sipped his tea. This had always been his favourite place to come and relax. It had been a couple of weeks since Sam and Alice had investigated a string of murders in London's east end, inadvertently landing Sam on a list of suspects when the police learned he hadn't been sent by Scotland Yard after all. *This is the thanks I get for banishing a murderous entity*, Sam had thought when he first saw the photofit approximation of his face on the news, *it's not my fault they were expecting the killer to be human.*

Thankfully, the police never knew his true identity, and after almost two weeks of only leaving the house to make a few stealthy, disguised runs to the corner shop (as well as a few cloaking spells for good measure) Sam was starting to feel confident that he wasn't in any immediate danger. The news had pretty much forgotten the whole thing after a couple of days, after all, and he'd had no trouble with the authorities since. He decided, rather wistfully as he gazed up at the cloudy skies above Hampstead, that he could take this time to sit and drink his tea in peace. So he did.

For the rarest of moments, Sam was able to relax and forget all of the burdens of his life, of the ghosts and demons and other paranormal phenomena he had to regularly deal with in his weird world. He idly thought about calling Alice for a friendly chat, maybe invite her out for dinner, and the idea of something so perfectly normal in his far from normal life made him smile. He sat back in the café's chair, contented. For once, Sam Hain could enjoy his cup of tea and not worry about anything out of the ordinary happening at all.

Only a few short moments later, probably no more than a minute or two, two men had entered the café and sat down a few tables away from Sam. The men wore identical black suits, clearly expertly tailored, with slim-style silk ties. Their eyes were covered by narrow pairs of sunglasses, the lenses seemingly opaque and as black as their suits. They both appeared to be in their forties, their faces worn and chiselled like stone. One of them was tall and slender, his short hair slicked back with more gel than was probably needed, while the other was slightly shorter and stockier, his hair thin and receding. Sam had thought very little of them at the time, not giving them more than a cursory glance as they'd sat down.

However, now that they were following him down the street, he cursed himself for daring to relax. He thought back to how they'd entered the café, and realised they hadn't even ordered anything. They had simply walked in, sat down at a nearby table and stared ahead in complete silence – both of them had been facing him, and he couldn't seem to remember hearing them talk to each other – and now there they were, no more than ten feet behind him, following him down the road.

Maybe I'm just overthinking things, Sam thought to himself as he quickened his pace. *It's the middle of the day, what harm can they do?* He took a quick glance over his shoulder. There they were, the two men in their well-tailored suits and eyes concealed by dark glasses, walking in eerily perfect unison. *Don't be so paranoid, why would they be following you?*, he tried to assure himself, but he couldn't shake the uneasy feeling. He rounded the corner onto a cobbled alleyway, grey brick buildings enclosing the narrow passage ahead of him. *Secret service? Demonic possession? Two men who really dislike my hat? Oh Christ…*

About half-way up the alleyway, Sam leaned against the wall and waited, his eyes trained on the corner from which he had just come. If they were following him, he thought, they'd turn into this alleyway too. If not, and this had all been sheer coincidence and utterly unnecessary paranoia, they would walk on past without even glancing in his direction. He wanted it to be the latter, he wanted them to just walk past so he could carry on with his day, but he had a sneaking suspicion that that would not be the case. It wasn't long until the two men came into view, and Sam's heart sank. They turned the corner and stood staring at him. Moving away from the wall as calmly and casually as he could manage, feeling like he was about to be in a Wild West style shootout, Sam tipped his fedora hat towards the two men. They both nodded back at him in unnatural unison.

'Oh, good,' Sam said under his breath, 'they are following me.' Turning around, he continued to walk up the alleyway, gradually walking faster and faster until, before he knew it, he'd broken into a run.

His feet pounded the cobbled street as he ran, carrying him forward as if by a will of their own. His greatcoat billowed out behind him, and Sam would probably have enjoyed how dramatic he must have looked in that moment were it not for his sudden rush of fear and adrenaline. Behind him he could hear two sets of feet starting to run in pursuit. He tried not to think of the two men chasing him down. He thought he had seen the bulge of a gun concealed beneath each of their jackets, but maybe in his panic he was now just imagining things. He was running blindly, no escape plan, no idea where to go other than somewhere where they weren't. Another side alley was coming up on his right, and he turned into it without a moment's thought.

A busy antique's market filled up most of the street. *Bollocks.* He kept on running, weaving his way through the crowd of shoppers browsing the stalls, hazarding a quick glance behind him every now and again. The men were still in pursuit, but the throngs of people antiquing were getting in their way. One of the men thrust an elderly woman out of his way as he charged through the crowd, sending her staggering into a display of 1920's china teacups. There was an audible gasp from several people, followed by the sound of smashing crockery. Neither of the men stopped or even turned around. They just carried on moving forwards.

Ducking into another passageway (some of the side routes in London can be fantastically long and labyrinthine), Sam hid himself amongst the bins in what was presumably the back courtyard of a shop. It was dank and unpleasant, and the smell coming from the bins would normally have made him retch. He was too fixated on hiding to notice the stench. If they found him there, he had no way of escape; they'd have him cornered. As much as he wanted to know who they were and why they were following him, he had a feeling he didn't want to find out on their terms. A trickle of sweat ran down the side of his face.

Peering from between two large black bins, Sam looked out into the courtyard. It seemed empty, but as he moved to get a slightly better view he could see them. The two men jogged around the corner and into the courtyard, their ties flopping as they ran, and came to an abrupt stop. They stood stock still, surveying the area. Sam held his breath, desperate not to make even the slightest of sounds. He felt his entire body tense up.

The two men stood there for a while, their bodies motionless but their heads slowly turning as they looked around, like eerie sentinels. It felt like an eternity had passed for Sam, but after just over a minute one of the men put his finger to his ear, pressing on a wireless earpiece. He nodded a single stoic nod, and the two men turned and strode out of the courtyard, rounding the corner and walking out of sight.

Sam Hain breathed a sigh of relief, emerging from amongst the bins and dusting himself off. *Bloody hell...*

CHAPTER I

'Okay,' Rachel said as she paced around the living room, swapping her phone from one ear to the other. 'Yeah, yeah, sure. That sounds good to me. Okay, cool, we'll see you there. By-e!' She hung up, slipping her phone into the back pocket of her jeans.

'So what's the plan for tonight then?' Alice asked. She leaned over the back of the sofa, twisting around to face Rachel.

'We're going to meet the rest of the girls at the Red Lion, probably catch a show or something, have a few drinks and go from there,' Rachel said. 'Sound good to you?'

'Sure, what've they got on this evening?'

'Didn't say. Probably just casual stuff. Knowing Chantelle, she'll be in a low-cut dress and caked in fake tan, the tart!' Rachel cackled.

'No, not the girls. The Red Lion. What've they got on this evening, show-wise?'

'Oh. I don't know. Some fringe performance art thing, I think.'

'Right,' Alice mused. 'What time are we heading out?'

'About eight.'

'Okay. Afterwards we could head to-' Alice was cut off mid-sentence as her phone vibrated loudly. 'One sec.' The phone vibrated again. She instinctively slid her thumb across the screen and tapped her messages.

Constantine Road. Come as soon as you can if you're free. -SH, read the first message. *Actually, free or not, come anyway. It's important*, read the second. Alice put the phone down on the arm of the sofa as she stood up, glancing around for her shoes.

'After the Lion we could head to the Steam Passage,' Alice finished, 'it looks like quite a nice place for a quiet drink.'

'Yeah, we can do.' Rachel nodded in agreement as she too started flipping through the notifications on her phone.

'Anyway, I'm heading out for a little bit,' Alice said, slipping on her converse shoes. She flicked and gently tousled her hair in front of the mirror.

'Alright, where are you off to?'

'Just going to meet a friend in Hampstead. I'll be back in time to get ready for tonight.'

'Okay, see you later, then. Have fun!' Rachel gave a little wave as Alice threw on her denim jacket and walked out of the door.

Alice had been thinking about going for a walk anyway, she wasn't one for staying in the flat all day, and paying a visit to Sam was more than enough of a good reason to head out for a while. She'd never seen his house before, and she didn't know what she should expect from the home of a man whose life was far from normal. The thought of it and what peculiar oddities lay within made her curious to say the least.

The weather that day was, contrary to the forecast, surprisingly pleasant. It wasn't warm by any stretch of the imagination, as the winter wasn't yet ready to yield to spring, but the air no longer carried with it a biting chill. However, Alice did have to pull her jacket tightly around herself to brace against a particularly brisk gust of wind. The sky was grey and overcast, but peaking out from between the thick grey clouds, Alice could see glimmers of blue sky beyond.

As she walked along the road towards Islington high street, Alice noticed that the trees lining the road were beginning to look a little greener, and the first new buds were starting to sprout. After the long, cold months of winter, the world was slowly coming back to life. Spring was just around the corner, she could feel it. Alice had always considered herself a spring spirit, preferring that sweet spot between the cold winter months and baking summer heat. It made the world feel fresh and full of life.

The tube, on the other hand, was not, and could never have been described as 'fresh' or 'full of life' even at the best of times. As Alice boarded the train at Highbury and Islington station she was immediately greeted by the stale air of the carriage, and she began to glance around for a free seat with as few stains as possible (which is a challenge easier said than done). As it turned out, she didn't need to look far, as the carriage was almost entirely empty; there were only two other people on board, both of whom had their heads down, reading the Metro with bored expressions on their faces.

The train jolted and lurched awkwardly as it pulled away from the platform, causing Alice to ungracefully stumble forward and into a seat, almost spilling the chai latte she'd picked up on the way to the station. She took a sip of the thick drink and grimaced as she tried to work out quite how she felt about it. On the one hand, it was sickly-sweet and creamy, and on the other it was quite spicy with decidedly more than a hint of cinnamon. The aftertaste was less than desirable, so she took another gulp, only to repeat the cycle. However, she found it to be a bit nicer this time, and concluded it was probably an acquired taste.

It was a relatively short journey to Hampstead Heath station, and before she'd even had time to untangle her headphones, Alice found herself stepping off of the train and onto the platform. The gate beeped merrily and swung open as Alice brushed her Oyster card against the scanner and, walking through the expectantly open gate, she made her way out of the station. Sam's flat was only a short walk from the station, and this was probably one of the rare occasions when Sam would say something was 'literally around the corner' and it actually was; as opposed to a mile or two away, which was more often the case.

Alice walked out onto South End Road,

passing the small fruit and vegetable stand which sat immediately outside of the station's entrance, and she started to head down the road. People were milling about the local cafés and shops, several others were walking their dogs towards the heath, and a surprising number of red buses seemed to be chasing each other around the pedestrian island towards the end of the road. Despite this part of Hampstead more closely resembling a small village, it was alive with city life.

Passing the corner shop at the end of the road, Alice turned left and began to walk along the rows of red brick houses on Constantine Road until, halfway down the road, she reached the address that Sam had given her. The doorway was up a set of concrete steps, framed by a wild growth of ivy which wound its way up the pillar one side of the door, across the wall above the door frame, and down the pillar on the other side. A large concrete dragon sat at the foot of the steps, proudly holding a shield between its talons. Had she been in any doubt this was the right address, Alice felt this was a bit of a give-away. She walked up to the door and knocked.

The door tentatively began to open, and through the widening gap the face of Sam Hain could be seen peering out. 'Oh good, it's you,' he said with a smile the instant he saw it was Alice, and he swung the door wide open to let her in.

'Hello,' Alice said with a sweet smile, and she quickly wiped her feet on the doormat as she stepped inside. The hallway ran the full length of the house, all white walls and cream carpet, and Alice was surprised that a man as unusual as Sam would have such a conservative taste in decor. Two doors ran off from the right side of the hall, and two staircases - one heading to the first floor, the other down to the basement - were at the far end of the hall. The house was a lot bigger than she'd first expected from the outside 'How do you afford to live in a place like this?' She asked, almost incredulously. Judging by the size of it alone it had to be an expensive property, doubly so considering its location so close to Hampstead Heath.

'He doesn't,' came the voice of a particularly stern-sounding woman from one of the doorways, presumably leading to the living room. 'He's already two months behind on the rent.'

Sam looked up at the ceiling and visibly rolled his eyes. 'Landlady,' he said dryly, 'I rent the basement flat.' He leaned towards the living room door and called out, 'all things in due time!' The voice from the living room didn't reply.

'Right then,' Sam announced, before lowering his voice to almost a whisper, 'I think I'm on to something big, and you're going to have to try not to think I've gone mad.' His eyes were suddenly wider and wilder than usual. Then, as if he'd just flicked a switch, he returned to normal. He clapped his hands together. 'But first, I'm going to have a cup of tea. Do you want anything?'

Alice nodded uncertainly. 'Okay... I'm feeling a little bit nervous now! But yeah, please, a cup of tea sounds perfect,' she said.

'Okay, two teas, coming up. My temple is just downstairs,' Sam said, and he began to lead the way down the stairs at the far end of the hallway. As she walked past the open door, Alice glanced in to say hello to the landlady, but all she saw was the back of a white-haired woman's head, happily occupied watching a daytime soap opera.

Alice followed Sam down the steep, bare-wooden staircase. She could see a single door at the bottom, a wooden pentagram hanging on the front of it, and a brass plaque in the very centre of the door which read 'Sam Hain - Occult Detective.' A large wooden sign rested above the door frame, emblazoned with the words *Abandon hope, all ye who enter here*, which Alice thought wasn't the most welcoming of signs.

'Here we are, then,' Sam said, producing a large, rustic-looking iron key from his pocket and turning the lock. He swung the door open and started to make his way towards another door at the back, which presumably lead to the kitchen. 'Make yourself at home, I'll be back in a minute.'

The door opened on to the middle of a fairly large room with bare, dark oaken floorboards and faded dark turquoise walls, mottled and marked with age and wear over the years. Alice stepped through the door and immediately found a creaky floorboard. To the left of the entrance was what looked like the dining room; an oak table with four chairs positioned around it sat perfectly in the middle of that half of the space, with a wrought iron candleholder twisting around itself in the centre of the table. To the right was the living room, where a worn looking sofa and mismatching arm chair were at right-angles to each other, sat on the nearest corner of an ancient looking rug. A coffee table stood in the middle of the rug, directly between the sofa and a fireplace. Diagonally across from the door was the television, covered in dust.

The walls were lined with tall, dark wood bookcases which seemed to overlook the entire room, looking as aged and worn as the walls and floorboards. On a number of the shelves were strange ornaments and artefacts, but most were packed beyond capacity with numerous books, piled up and crammed in however they would fit, with tomes and volumes the likes of which Alice had never seen before. There were, of course, some more recognisable pieces of literature - a handful of contemporary books, a number of classics - but there was also a generous amount of slightly more obscure titles.

The room didn't look decrepit by any means, but nor was it pristine. It put Alice in mind of a mysterious old house with a peculiar twinge of Victorian and Gothic design. She hadn't really known what to expect from Sam's taste in interior design, but she wasn't too surprised by it. What did surprise her was the size of the place. The room she was standing in inexplicably seemed to be larger than the ground floor, and a number of doors leading from the dining room suggested that Sam's basement flat ran off into even more rooms.

Alice made her way into the living room area

and, out of curiosity, she decided to have a quick flick through some of the more unusual books on Sam's shelves while she waited for him.

The Magical Creatures Bestiary was the first volume she pulled off of a shelf. The book contained an exhaustive list of fairy tale animals, lovingly illustrated and filled with information about various kinds of magical creatures, some of which Alice could faintly recall from childhood bedtime stories. Next to this was something titled *How to Bag a Jabberwock*, a practical guide to monster hunting – also illustrated – which didn't focus so much on the fairy tale element as much as it did on the hunting of mythical creatures, as though jabberwocks and manticores and werewolves were game for some fantasy blood-sport. There was also a hefty tome of almost encyclopedic lengths, *A Guide to the Supernatural World*, which was presumably about everything metaphysical (some items in the guide had had their paragraphs scribbled over, and Sam's handwriting scrawled next to it brazenly exclaiming '*WRONG!*'). The shelf below was littered with an array of magickal works, including books by Aleister Crowley and John Dee, and a red leather-bound volume called *A Guide to High Magick*. Something about these books seemed almost sacred. Enchanted.

On the wooden coffee table in the middle of the room sat the familiar sight of Sam's self-penned guide to all things weird, the book Alice had once referred to as 'Demonology for Dummies.' An ink-pot and black feathered quill sat next to it, and as Alice opened the book she found that on the first page Sam had written in calligraphic style the words *Encyclopedia Arcanica*. She nodded approvingly, thinking the title had a slightly more respectable sound to it than her unofficial one, and flicked through the pages. She noticed he'd made a few amendments to some of the previous entries. She suspected that he often needed to make revisions to what he thought he knew; there was bound to be no shortage of surprises when it came to the weird and wonderful world in which Sam lived.

After quickly flicking through the *Encyclopedia Arcanica*, Alice put the book down and glanced over towards the fireplace. She thought she saw something glinting on the mantelpiece out of the corner of her eye, and when she turned her attention to it she saw the mantelpiece was adorned with an array of strange and abnormal looking things she couldn't even begin to fathom, odd twisting ornaments and alien-looking artefacts. The particular thing which had caught Alice's eye was a clear quartz crystal skull, glistening in a beam of sunlight which was coming in through a small gap at the top of the window where the street-level was just about visible. Compared to some of the other things on display (including several stones engraved with unusual runes, statues of strange figures she didn't recognise, and an old, spherical glass pocket watch), the crystal skull wasn't the most outlandish thing in the room. Alice picked it up. It was a weighty thing, made of solid crystal and just the right size for her to hold comfortably in one hand. She gently stroked its perfectly smooth surface with her thumbs before putting it back down.

Hanging above the mantelpiece, stuck in place with tape and blue-tac, were several sheets of paper covering a large portion of the wall. They'd been arranged to form one large, abnormally-shaped, sheet. The paper was covered in scrawled notes and printed-out images, pen marks linking point to point to point. One piece, towards the top of the would-be mind-map, had a picture of a dark cobbled street, the date *31st OCTOBER 2013* written in block capitals above the picture. *The night I first met Sam...* Alice mused. A number of almost illegible notes referencing the veil between words were scrawled around the date, as well as a couple of photographs of eerily dark and empty streets and unearthly shadowy forms. *Darkness is coming?* was written by the side of it.

The words *darkness is coming* recurred quite a few times across the pieces of paper, along with a photograph of the Void crystal they'd found in the loft on their night in Knightsbridge (notably missing from the artefacts on display in the room), two images of the late Joe Norton, both when he was alive and with his severed head in the Grimditch butcher's shop window, and numerous notes about Sam's methods used in fending off 'shadow eels' and a 'pig-headed demon.' There were sub-notes attached to these, reminding Sam to come up with better names for them. At the centre of all of the pieces of paper, in the very heart of the arrangement, was a map of central

London. Sam had marked each location where these previous cases had taken place, circling where they'd been. Islington, Knightsbridge, Grimditch... There were also some other marks across the map, small crosses presumably marking some of Sam's other exploits.

As Alice took a step forward to take a closer look at Sam's notes, she felt something beneath her feet. It was smooth and cold, but wasn't the marble tiling surrounding the fireplace; it felt rounded, and irregularly shaped. She took a step back and looked down. At her feet was an intricate pattern of two concentric circles, formed by the even and symmetrical placement of crystals. Orange, black and teal stones formed the circles, with quartz points facing outwards in all directions leading out from the centre like the spokes of a wheel. A single larger piece of quartz stood in the middle of the pattern. Leaning against this central stone was the metallic, shiny wand-like shape of Sam's transphasic energy probe. Or TechnoWand, as Alice still liked to think of it.

'Careful,' came Sam's voice from somewhere behind her, as if he was warning a child from something dangerous, 'try not to disturb the grid too much. It keeps the Thing away.'

Alice turned to look at him, a puzzled expression on her face. 'What's 'the Thing'?'

'I don't know. I just call it 'the Thing.'' Sam widened his eyes as if to convey a sense of awe and mystery, but it simply came off as cartoonish.

He raised a cup of tea up as he made his way

over, and sat himself in the armchair. She made her way back over to him, taking the tea and sitting down on the sofa. It may have looked old and worn, but it was surprisingly comfortable. She took a sip from her cup, and made the satisfied 'ah' sound people make when they take the first sip of a good cup of tea.

'So, why will I think you've gone mad this time?' Alice asked. She sounded almost blasé about it.

'I think I'm being followed,' Sam confided. Of all the things he'd said since they first met, Alice thought, this was possibly the sanest.

'By who? Or what?' Alice leaned forward, intrigued. Her mind immediately jumped to thoughts of demons and dark spirits.

'Men in Black,' was Sam's simple reply.

'Like the Will Smith movie?'

'I'm not joking, Alice. The Men in Black are after me.' His face was the sincerest Alice had ever seen it, and she thought she detected a hint of fear behind his otherwise stoic eyes.

'Okay,' she said slowly, 'why are they after you?'

'I don't know,' Sam said, and his voice seemed to quaver, 'I don't know...'

'You don't think it might be because you impersonated a police officer to gain access to a murder scene? The authorities might have assigned agents to find you. One of those photo-fit thingies of your face was on the news. They want anyone who knows anything about you to come forward.'

'I know. Thankfully I've been able to lay relatively low, and know a few things about keeping anonymous. Hiding in plain sight, that sort of thing. But no. No. Even if it were, they wouldn't be quite so... Creepy.' He couldn't think of any other word to describe them. The two men in Hampstead had had a decidedly creepy air about them when they'd been following him, distant and almost ethereal, as if they were part of an entirely different world than the rest of the town. Were it not for the old woman and all the broken crockery, he would wonder if anyone else would have noticed them.

'What makes you think they're after you? You might just be paranoid.'

'I'm not paranoid. I thought I was, but they've been following me,' he said, and he leaned in closer to her. 'Alice, listen. I don't know who or what I can trust any more. I don't even know how safe I am in my own town. I can count the people I trust on one hand.' He held up his right hand and waggled his fingers about a bit, before reaching for his cup of tea. 'You're one of them, by the way.' She knew he meant it.

'Who do you think they are, these Men in Black?'

Sam gulped down a mouthful of tea and sighed, placing his cup back down and clasping his hands together. He rested his chin on his clasped hands and stared off into the middle-distance. 'I really don't know. Secret service, maybe. They looked the government type. MI-5, MI-6...' He unclasped his hands, and began to drum his fingers impatiently on the table as he thought. 'The thing is, with everything I've been looking into, we could soon find ourselves in something far deeper than I could have imagined.'

'What do you mean?' Alice asked.

'The Regents,' Sam stated.

Alice immediately thought back to the events at Grimditch. The corpses, the esoteric symbols and the hint of a cult all came flashing back through her mind. They had discovered that a group called the Regents had been connected to the events in some way, but that was all they knew. Who the Regents were, what they do, and how they were involved still remained a mystery. The unwelcome memories of Grimditch and the decapitated body nauseated Alice, and the image of the entity wearing the body of Pete Jones with the head of a pig made her feel sick to the pit of her stomach. Whenever she thought of Grimditch, the thoughts would grip her mind like a vice; it would take a long time for her to forget. She shuddered involuntarily, and broke herself out of the traumatic trance.

'I've been trying to do some digging to find out anything I can about them,' Sam carried on talking, seemingly oblivious Alice had spaced out for a moment, 'but I haven't been able to find anything remotely informative. I've asked an old friend to help, he was always more knowledgeable about cults and secret societies. He'll have access to the right information. He should be joining us shortly.'

As if on cue, there was the sound of feet coming down the creaking stairs shortly followed by a knock at the door. Before Sam could stand up to answer it, the door opened and a man in a grey twill suit with a satchel slung over his shoulder walked in. His hair was shorter and more controlled than Sam's (that was hardly difficult), and Alice estimated he was probably in his late twenties. She couldn't really tell, though; guessing people's ages wasn't something she considered to be her strong point.

'Alright, Sam,' said the man as he closed the door behind him.

'Good to see you, James,' Sam replied, standing up and walking over to greet his visitor. He held his hand out to shake, but his greeting was met with a fist. James held his arm outstretched, fist clenched, anticipating Sam to reciprocate with a fist-bump. The two stood stock still, staring at one another wordlessly, their arms extended towards each other with mismatching gestures, waiting for the other to do the same. James gave a nonchalant shrug of the head, and Sam yielded, scrunching his open hand into a fist and gently punching James's.

'Hi,' said Alice once the whole awkward greeting had concluded.

'James, this is Alice. Alice, meet James Mortimer,' Sam said, waving his hands chaotically between the two of them as way of introduction.

James Mortimer was a tall and brooding man with a name to match. He stood probably a couple of inches taller than Sam and had a vaguely intimidating presence about him, but not in the same kind of way so frequently referenced in erotic novels. Alice held out her clenched fist, but instead of another fist-bump James delicately took her hand, unfurled her fingers and gave her a quick peck on the back of the hand.

'So you're Sam's new protégée I've heard so much about. A pleasure,' he said with a smile. She wasn't too sure how she felt about being called a 'protégée', but she decided she'd let it slide just this once.

'Good to meet you,' Alice reciprocated, 'I've heard literally nothing about you.'

'Oh, come on, Sam, my man! You mean to tell me you haven't shared the stories of our most excellent adventures?' He turned to face his old friend with a look of mock offence.

'What, like the time we found an enchanted mirror and you were convinced you were the... Oh, how did you put it? 'The fairest of them all'?' Sam smirked and raised an eyebrow at his old friend.

'Not the stupid ones, the exciting ones! Remember Manor House?'

'We said we'd never talk about Manor House again,' Sam said, forcing his face into the most serious expression he could manage and speaking with a tone so stern it would be the envy of any middle school teacher. James and Sam then solemnly nodded at each other in unison, suppressing the urge to smile at their stupid performance.

'Anyway,' James announced, pulling a tablet computer out of his satchel and flicking his finger across the screen, 'to business.' He sat on the sofa next to Alice as he continued to poke and prod at the tablet, opening files and sliding documents around the screen. 'I've been researching those Regents you mentioned, Sam.'

Sam slowly sat back down in the armchair and leaned forward. 'And? What did you find?'

'Not a lot,' James said distantly, his focus still on the screen, 'officially, they don't exist.'

'They bloody do!' Sam interjected before slowly sinking back into his armchair, realising that his outburst probably made him appear more paranoid than he already was. 'I have the files from the Grimditch case…'

'Exactly, officially they may not exist,' James continued, 'but there are several accounts of them and their activities. At first, I thought they may have just been a small-time cult, but talk among conspiracy circles implies they're much bigger.'

'As in, above the government?' Sam asked.

'Quite possibly,' James nodded, 'certain reports I've seen from conspiracy theorists suggest the rabbit hole goes much, much deeper. Some believe they're a governmental department for paranormal research, others that they are entwined with or even above the government, influencing events as they see fit.' He poked at the screen and pulled up a file. 'There are a number of occult symbols associated with them, which apparently surround their places of operation. The All-Seeing Eye, Torch of Prometheus, that sort of thing. One account even depicts the same symbol you found in connection with them.'

Alice and Sam peered over his shoulder to take a look. On the screen was a shape they both recognised; an angular hieroglyph with a right-slanting line at the top, and a long vertical line stretching downwards, ending in a two-pronged fork shape. The Was Sceptre. The symbol of the clandestine Regents.

'Yeah. That's the one,' Sam said.

'At this point, I'd take anything we find with a pinch of salt, though. This guy claims he was involved in something called the Voidwalker Project, supposedly they were sending test subjects through quantum gateways. Allegedly, many of the test subjects were driven mad,' James shrugged. 'His report reads like the ultimate conspiracy theory; he even says that any information leaks are suppressed, whistleblowers are silenced, and the Men in Black tie up their loose ends through any means necessary.'

'If that's the case, how did this person share this information?' Alice asked. She was sceptical at the best of times, especially when it came to crackpot conspiracy theories, but then again she didn't believe in ghosts and demons until she met Sam.

'Like I say, pinch of salt,' James said casually.

'Plausible deniability,' Sam muttered almost as if he was only talking to himself. He stared at the coffee table with a far-off gaze in his eyes.

'What do you mean?' James asked, looking at his friend with concern.

'Plausible deniability,' Sam repeated. 'The Regents don't officially exist, right? So they must keep a tight lid on things to keep the truth of their existence from getting out, silencing leaks and deleting information. But they let the most out-there theories slip. The most unhinged voices are heard. They eliminate the legitimate threats, and the remaining leaks are branded the ramblings of a madman, or works of fiction, and they fall into obscurity. Anyone who winds up believing it simply gets labelled as another crazy. If anyone suspects anything, they can point to these theories and state they're nothing more than paranoid delusions.'

'That rant is a prime example!' James said jokingly, but Sam did not seem amused.

'James, this morning I was enjoying a perfectly good cup of tea, and ended up being chased by men in very good looking black suits,' Sam said in a very serious tone. 'You say that account said that the Men in Black come to tie up the loose ends? There is no doubt in my mind that that is exactly what I was running from. After everything involving the Regents surrounding Grimditch, I wouldn't be surprised if my,' he paused and looked at Alice, '*our* involvement stepped on a few toes.'

James nodded silently. His friendship with Sam Hain went back to their college days. As a couple of teenagers, they'd dabbled in the occult and they and a group of their friends used to go ghost hunting in abandoned houses and cemeteries. Sam had gone down the route of magick, investigating the paranormal and demon hunting, while James had been more interested in researching the history and influence of secret societies and cult practices. Their interests in the esoteric may have diverged, but they both respected each other's expertise, and sometimes their two worlds would converge. Now, James thought, could be one of those moments.

'Okay,' he eventually said, putting down his tablet and meeting Sam's gaze, 'if the Men in Black are looking for you and you really have caught the attention of the Regents, you're going to have to lay low until we know what's really going on.'

Alice had remained quiet all of this time, listening to the two of them discussing the conspiracy of the Regents, and she was trying to get her head around the madness of what they were saying. It all sounded so ludicrous, and if any of it was true it was almost too huge to comprehend. She'd witnessed the paranormal with her own eyes, she'd spoken with spirits and she'd stood alongside Sam as he fought off dark entities. In a way, she could almost believe that an esoteric supernatural organisation was pulling the strings from behind the curtains; certainly, she could think of quite a few politicians who seemed to be anything other than human, and it wouldn't come as much of a surprise to her if she were to learn that a handful of them were beings from another dimension. But to consider that she and Sam might be involved in a conspiracy with an organisation beyond government jurisdiction seemed unreal, and more than a little bit frightening.

'Try clearing your name,' she said, and both Sam and James looked at her quizzically. 'If you go to the police and clear your name, maybe the MiB will get off your back? You didn't do anything wrong-'

'I impersonated a police investigator to gain access to evidence in a murder case,' Sam interrupted, 'which they'd see as potentially perverting the course of justice. Especially when they haven't got any solid evidence to identify the killer, largely because it wasn't from this particular plane of existence.'

Alice looked at the floor for a moment. 'I see your point,' she said, 'I'm at a loss for ideas, then.'

'And what if it was the Regents who put me on the list of suspects in the first place? If they're above the police, and they know about what happened, maybe they want to bring me in and silence me,' Sam stared at Alice and James with wild eyes. 'If their ranks really do go as high up as the government, or beyond, then we're all just puppets to them. But people like us see the world for how it really is. We have no strings for them to pull. So they come after us, to shut us up or make sure we don't get in the way of their games.'

Alice stared at him, unblinking. For the briefest of moments, she thought that he had completely lost it. Perhaps he was losing the ability to distinguish between the world he knew and the rest of the... Well, it wasn't so much the real world as it was the 'normal' world (the metaphysical world is just as real as plants and animals and mortgages, but decidedly more interesting and fantastical and entirely not normal). Maybe he was starting to see the demons everywhere, even where they weren't.

'See, I thought you'd think I was mad,' Sam said, his eyes darting between her's as if he was scanning her, reading her thoughts. 'I don't need you to believe me, Alice, I just need you to trust me. I don't know what they want with me, but they could very well come for you too. Just be on your guard. Please.'

Alice nodded silently, and she leaned forward, taking his hand in hers. 'As mad as this all sounds – and it really does sound absolutely bloody bonkers – I trust you. I do.'

Sam's face turned into the picture of relief, as if a great weight had been lifted off of his shoulders. 'Thank you,' he simply said. 'If I'm right, I dread to think what they might want from me. From us. And I hate the thought of anything happening to you.'

Alice nodded understandingly.

'Listen,' James said sombrely, 'we don't even really know what we're dealing with yet. The little information I've been able to scrape together about the Regents could just be the ramblings of another crazed conspiracy theorist. Just lay low, watch your backs, and don't do anything stupid.' He slid his tablet back into his satchel and zipped up its pouch. 'I'll keep digging. All we can do is try to get to the bottom of this, and hope that we find the answer before the answer finds us.'

CHAPTER II

The weather had taken a turn that evening. Gone were the light skies and gentle breezes, instead replaced with a torrential downpour and rolling dark clouds looming over the city. The rain drops fell thick and fast. The skies turned black.

As she walked back alone in the heavy rain, Alice's mind wandered to Sam's ranting about the Regents. *Could he be right?*, she wondered, half considering it. She hadn't believed him about the supernatural and metaphysical entities when they'd first met, and had very quickly learned that it wasn't all as absurd as it had sounded. She wondered if it could be the same now, if the world really was being governed by hidden organisations directing things from behind the curtain.

It wasn't long before Alice was thoroughly drenched. Her mousy blonde hair turned brown in the downpour, and her clothes clung damp and heavy to her body. A cold wind blew down Constantine Road, but it felt like an arctic blast which cut through to the bone against her wet clothes. Alice ran her fingers through her rain-soaked hair and quickened her pace to the station.

'Need a lift?' Came a voice from somewhere

behind her, and she turned around to see a sleek black car pull up alongside her. The man behind the wheel had wound down the window, and was leaning out towards her. He was very well dressed, presumably driving home from work in some high-end job. 'You shouldn't be out getting drenched in weather like this.'

Alice politely declined the man's offer, saying she was heading for the tube and was only a minute or two from there. He insisted he give her a lift, or she'd catch her death of cold in this weather, but she assured him she'd dry off as soon as she got back home. The man had eventually driven off, although when Alice reached Hampstead Heath station she was sure she could see his car parked on the curb a little further up the road.

She stood beneath the shelter on the platform, huddled among the other disgruntled travellers trying to stay out of the rain. A few errant drops of water snuck through the roof of the shelter, landing in thick droplets on the heads of the people below. When the train arrived, Alice stepped onto the crowded carriage, cold and completely soaked through. She squeezed herself into a small gap in amongst a throng of similarly drenched Londoners. As the train began to move, she grabbed a hold of the pole and resigned herself to standing and waiting for Highbury and Islington.

Sam had left the house for just a few moments to buy some food for that evening. Out of simplicity, he'd headed to the Mark's and

Spencer's no more than a ten minute walk away to buy one of their ready-made vegetable lasagne. It took him twenty minutes to walk it, as, owing to his paranoia, he'd taken a less than direct route to avoid being followed.

He wondered, as he peered over someone's shoulder into the freezer compartment, whether he was being too paranoid. Maybe he was seeing things where they weren't (reading about cults and conspiracies can do that sometimes). He thought about the men in the tailored suits, and how they'd followed him and chased him through the side-alleys of Hampstead. There was no doubt that they were after him, and he knew that he was better off being on his guard than being too complacent. He started to think about Alice, and wondered if she had got back home okay. He decided that when he got back home, he'd text her to make sure she was safe and sound. Or was that a bit excessive?

'Unexpected Item in Bagging Area.'

He sighed, removed the lasagna, stared at the screen impatiently and replaced it on the checkout.

'Unexpected Item in Bagging Area.'

He muttered a series of irate-sounding words at the machine, and tapped at the touch screen with so much force he may as well have been punching it. Today was no longer a day he felt comfortable being out of the house unless it was absolutely necessary, and now it seemed that the self-service checkout was conspiring against him.

'Please wait. Help is on the way.'

What if it actually was conspiring against him? *You're getting paranoid, now*, Sam told himself as he stared at the machine, waiting. *Or am I?* He told himself to focus, to stay calm and buy his lasagna. He would be home in less than ten minutes, put his dinner in the oven, and sit down to see what was on TV that evening. A simple M&S checkout wasn't going to push him over the edge.

The sound of footsteps coming closer and closer reached his ears, and Sam turned around to see one of the members of staff approaching him. She was in her late teens, dressed head-to-toe in company-issued clothes and looking almost swamped by her fleece. She flashed him a well-trained customer service smile, while her eyes remained emotionless and unchanging. 'How can I help, sir?' She asked.

'Unexpected Item in Bagging Area,' the checkout machine chimed in helpfully.

'It's been rigged,' Sam said plainly.

'Rigged, sir? I'm sure there's just a mistake. Let me just-' She was about to override the machine's warning message, but Sam interrupted her.

'It's been rigged to hold me up and delay me… But you already knew that, didn't you?' Sam's eyes narrowed as he inspected the assistant, who stared back at him with a mixture of fear and confusion.

'I… Sorry?'

'You're one of *them*, aren't you?' A voice in the back of his mind told him he was being irrational, but he ignored it. The assistant stared back at him, perplexed, and she leaned around Sam to fix the machine. It was then that she spotted the problem.

'Sir, you've left your wallet in the bagging area. You're the unexpected item.' She smiled again to try and lighten the situation.

Sam looked down and saw his wallet sitting alongside the lasagna, and his face flushed a rather vivid shade of red. He looked sheepishly back at the assistant, muttered a 'sorry' and a 'thank you', and desperately tried to pretend he hadn't just made an arse of himself.

A cheer rose up from the crowd filling the theatre above the Old Red Lion. The production had been a postmodern take on Romeo and Juliet, in which the same actor had played the parts of both Romeo and Juliet; supposedly as a statement on the character's (and presumably actor's) love of himself. The Montagues and Capulets were also played by the same group of actors, as a comment on the internal conflict caused by trying to raise such a troubled, narcissistic teenager. It was almost a good idea, in theory, but only almost. In execution it was entirely different.

The cheer from the audience was likely due to the fact that the play was over, not that the actors would ever know that. Their next production was to be a version of Hamlet, in which Hamlet is also his own father and his uncle.

Following the rest of the audience downstairs, Alice made her way into the pub below. It was relatively crowded downstairs, as the throng of the audience began to fill out the pub. It felt like a very traditional pub, with fading red carpets and mahogany furnishings, and the bar was alive with clientele clamouring for drinks. The general hubbub of a packed out bar filled the air, glasses chinked, and laughter and cheers soared above the chatter of the crowd. Alice walked up to the bar, standing beside Rachel, and ordered a bottle of passion fruit cider.

'So what'd you make of it?' Rachel asked, a quizzical eyebrow raising above her right eye.

'It was... Interesting,' Alice replied. It was the politest way she could describe the performance.

'Didn't understand a word of it, me!' Rachel said with a giggle, and she took a swig from her bottle of cider.

Alice's bottle of cider, along with a pint glass filled with ice, was placed in front of her. The golden liquid bubbled over the ice cubes as Alice poured her drink, and she took a sip of the sweet and refreshingly crisp beverage. She peered around to see where the other girls were, and could see Chantelle - with her platinum blonde hair and unseasonably tanned skin in a very tight and very low-cut red dress - heading towards a table in the corner, where Jess was already seated with her glass of chardonnay.

'Fancy coming clubbing with us in a bit?' Rachel leaned in towards Alice, and took another swig from her bottle. 'It's kind of boring here.'

Alice disagreed. She much preferred the

atmosphere of a good pub to the thumping music and eccentric light show of any club. She'd rather sit around chatting with friends over a few drinks than all of the shot-fuelled dancing and not being able to hear each other over the music. 'Nah,' she eventually said to Rachel, 'I'm not sure I'm really in the clubbing mood.'

'Oh go on, it'll be fun! Chantelle and I were saying how dull it is just to sit around, and then Jess said about this club night going on and-'

Rachel continued talking, but Alice had zoned out of the conversation, for just over Rachel's shoulder she'd noticed something. Two men in well-tailored suits had entered the pub, their thin black ties falling in a perfectly straight line down to their buttoned up slim-fit jackets. They both wore dark sunglasses which only covered their eyes, which was weird for ten o'clock on a Saturday night. As Alice surreptitiously watched them (it wasn't difficult; they stood out like sore thumbs in amongst the crowd of the pub), she noticed they didn't order a drink, or talk, or mingle. They simply walked in and sat down, facing in her direction. Something about the two of them made her feel incredibly uneasy.

One of the men turned to the other, and nodded silently. Neither of them moved their mouths to speak. That wasn't the only odd thing Alice noticed about them. They seemed to be entirely separate from everyone else in the pub, moving through the crowd unhindered, and simply looking at them their existence seemed to jar with the rest of reality. There was an otherworldly aura about them, almost as if they weren't quite as much a part of this world as they appeared.

'Actually, you know what, why the hell not?' Alice declared, not really sure whether Rachel was still explaining the club plan or not, and she clinked her drink against Rachel's before taking a big swig. 'We'll leave in five, yeah?'

She didn't care where they went, all Alice wanted was to get away from the men who had just entered. She couldn't shake the thought of what Sam had said earlier, and, she reasoned, heading to a packed club was a good place to lose them. If, indeed, they were following her.

It was pitch black in the alleyway. Sam peered cautiously around the corner and out onto the road, keeping himself pinned as close to the wall as possible, lurking just outside of the pools of light cast by the streetlamps. His hat was askew, his coat wet and marred with flecks of mud, and the vegetable lasagna in his Mark's and Spencer's bag was defrosted. Headlights veered around the corner, driving along the road in his direction, and Sam ducked back behind the wall. He flattened himself against it, and took a quick glance out of the corner of his eye. It was the nondescript black van again, driving slowly past.

He'd left the shop about two hours ago and started to head home when he'd noticed the two men in suits approaching. He'd doubled back inside, feigning he'd forgotten to buy something else, and kept a cautious eye out. Sure enough, the men in suits had entered too and seemed to follow him up and down the aisles from a discreet distance. He hmm'd over a bottle of cabernet sauvignon, checked the price of a packet of crisps, and was eventually able to lose them in the bakery section (managing to abscond with a cheese twist at the same time). He fled as quickly and casually as he could manage, and was back outside in no time.

However, it wasn't long before the two men were stood outside the shop, fingers pressed to their ears, presumably as something in their headsets spoke with them. They nodded in silent unison, and started to follow Sam down the road. Once again, he found himself quickening his pace. His mind raced as he worked out whether he could lose them and still get back home safely. The two men didn't bother to speed up to catch him, they simply followed Sam at a methodical and even pace. They looked similar to the men in the café, but he couldn't be sure whether they were the same agents.

But he knew they were agents. Men in Black. There was no doubt in his mind. Any doubts he had about whether something sinister was going on, any attempts his rational mind made to try and reassure him he was being paranoid, were dispelled. They were definitely still following him. He checked over his shoulder and there they were, striding after him with purpose. He carried on walking as fast as he could manage without having to break into a run. If he started to run from them, Sam thought, it would provoke them into giving chase, and he didn't foresee that ending in his favour. He wondered why they hadn't already done that, why they didn't just run after him and try to tackle him to the ground. The thought was quickly brushed aside; more than anything he was grateful that they hadn't made much of an effort to catch up with him. It bought him more time to plan his escape.

The familiar and normally safe sight of home was just across the road from him. The outside light had been left on, causing the green of the ivy around the door and the red brick wall to glow vibrantly in the darkening twilight. It was like a beacon calling out to him; a beacon he would have to ignore for the moment. He longed to be at home, relaxing in front of the TV, in the comfort of his living room, and - most importantly - not being followed by secret agents. But there was no way he could just walk up to the door and let himself in, not when they were tailing him. Sam put his head down and carried on walking, all the while his brain raced to think of a way he could try to lose them.

With the glaring of headlights and screeching of wheels, a black van pulled out of the road directly ahead of Sam, causing him to jump. In many ways it was a standard black transit van, although its tinted windows were entirely blacked out, and no license plates. The van took a sickening swerve around the corner and with the jolting of brakes it came to an abrupt stop alongside Sam. The side door clicked and began to slide open. Without a moment's hesitation, he ran.

Sam's feet pounded the pavement, his coat billowing out behind him in the wind and his boots splashing through the puddles. His face was drenched by running head-long into the rainfall. He no longer cared about remaining discreet, or whether he'd provoke them into further action. Running was his only chance. He glanced over his shoulder and saw the other two agents approach the van and jump into the back. Beaming white headlights loomed ominously across the street as the van made a U-turn, veering around to give chase, and with a sudden roar from the engine they were in pursuit. Now that their mark was on the run, they were picking up speed and rapidly closing the gap. Sam desperately prayed he'd be able to outrun and lose them.

It seemed that Sam's prayers were answered, as within moments he realised he was coming up to a footpath which lead over a bridge to Hampstead Heath. Darting to his left at an almost perfect right angle, Sam sprinted up and over the footbridge and carried on running out into Hampstead Heath, disappearing in the darkness of the dwindling daylight.

He didn't stop running for quite some time. Even though the van couldn't have pursued him over the footbridge, there was every chance the Men in Black would be following him on foot. Having bought himself maybe a few precious moments more by escaping over the bridge, Sam wasn't going to slow down until he'd put a good amount of distance between him and them. He carried on running up Parliament Hill, his legs throbbing with each laboured step and his breathing heavy and uneven, as much from exertion as anxiety. His boots were caked in the fresh mud of the heath, and his clothes were soaked from the rain. Sam stumbled into a copse of trees part-way up hill, and slumped down behind one of the trunks.

He had watched them from there, hidden behind the trees and concealed by the dark of night. His pursuers had indeed got out to follow him on foot, but evidently lost sight of him soon after the footbridge. They were still at the base of the hill, wandering around with their torches casting cones of light across the heath. The light from the torches never reached Sam; in his position, he was entirely out of sight. He watched them for ten minutes, although to Sam it felt infinitely longer, before he felt it safe to start making a move again. The agents were still lurking around where he had come from, but they were starting to slowly snake back towards Constantine Road.

It was not easy navigating Hampstead Heath in the dark. Sam had been here several times before, often absent-mindedly wandering around the park, but by night it was like treading the grounds of a familiar yet entirely unrecognisable world. His eyes had adjusted to the night as much as could be expected, but still he could barely see where he was going. He tripped and stumbled along in the pitch black, not daring to use his phone as a torch in case someone saw its light.

Rain pelted the already sodden earth, and the occasional arc of lightning streaked through the pitch black skies, briefly lighting up the way ahead with a distant growl of thunder. For almost an hour Sam Hain had wandered, venturing further into the heath than he'd intended, and after walking in a large, looping arc from Parliament Hill, Sam was nearing home again. Walking alongside a large pond, almost perfectly black beneath the night's sky, Sam had risked a glance at the map on his phone, and he discovered a shortcut through a small alleyway onto South Hill Park Gardens.

It was this alleyway he now found himself in. He watched as the black van disappeared out of sight, presumably to loop around again on a patrol. Not sure of when he'd next be presented with the opportunity, Sam made a mad dash around the corner and down the road. He was only a short distance from Hampstead Heath station now, and he would be home in five minutes if he made good pace. Stepping out onto the main street which ran past the station, Sam's heart was beating faster than ever. His eyes darted around, looking for any signs of the Men in Black. He hated feeling so exposed, but there was no other way than along the road. At least with other people on the street and a steady stream of passing cars and buses, Sam could try to disappear amongst the crowd, disguised beneath the canopy of rain-drenched umbrellas. Whenever he could, he would keep as far from the road as possible, taking a less visible route around to Constantine

Road.

It wasn't long before Sam was bounding up the steps to the front door. With shaking hands, he thrust his key into the lock and slipped inside, closing the door quickly behind him. His landlady wasn't in, and most of the lights were off, but he was home. Sam dropped the plastic bag to the floor; amidst the fleeing from the Men in Black, he had crammed the bag with the M&S lasagna into his coat pocket as best he could, and now what was meant to be his dinner was a horrible, defrosted and soggy mess. He leaned against the inside of the front door, slowly allowing himself to slide down it until he was sat on the floor, and let out a long, exasperated sigh.

The club was not even remotely what Alice had wanted from her Saturday night. The floor was sticky, the music obnoxiously loud, and the place was packed full with people dancing in a haze of energy drinks and alcohol, plus other substances. She and the girls had sat down at one of the tables towards the back of the club, and had tried to talk with each other over their drinks. It was mostly futile, no-one could hear each other over the music, unless they were literally screaming directly into each other's ears, and they eventually gave up on conversation.

Rachel had got up to dance, a slightly unbalanced dance, owing in part to her unnaturally high heels as well as the neon coloured shots she'd downed as soon as they had arrived. Alice watched with the fascinated curiosity of a wildlife expert watching a newborn giraffe learning to walk. She tottered around the dance floor, waving her arms and clearly having a fantastic time.

Chantelle followed shortly after her, taken by the hand and led away, giggling, by a particularly muscular and typically handsome man in his late-twenties. Her body wiggled seductively in her red dress as she followed the man, her hips swaying to the sound of the beat, before he scooped her up in his arms and swaggered to the centre of the dance floor.

The music thumped on, and multicoloured lights strobed and danced across the black silhouettes of the revelers in the dark of the club. Jess had excused herself and disappeared to find the toilets, leaving Alice sat at the table. She finished the last of her vodka and coke, and she toyed with the idea of getting another drink. She didn't feel drunk enough to jump in and start dancing yet, but if she was going to be here in this club anyway she may as well enjoy herself. Half-melted ice cubes clinked merrily as she vacantly swirled them around at the bottom of her glass.

'Can I buy you a drink?' A monotone shout came from somewhere to Alice's right, and she turned to see a man standing next to her. He looked at her and smiled a winning smile.

'Sorry?' Alice shouted back, leaning in a bit closer.

'Can. I. Buy. You. A. Drink?' The man repeated, making sure to speak slowly and loudly so she could hear him.

Alice looked back up at him, and she noticed that he was actually quite attractive; beneath spiky light brown hair, his face was chiseled and defined like a carving of a Greek god, with prominent high cheekbones complementing his strong jaw. A thin, perfectly trimmed subtle layer of stubble peppered his chin. Even in the dark she could see his opalescent blue eyes. Then she noticed something else. Beneath the cuff of his sleeve he had a small tattoo, and she was able to clock the rough shape of it before he adjusted his sleeve to hide it. It was a vertical line, a right-slanting line at its head, and two prongs at the bottom. She swallowed heavily as she felt a new bout of panic – or was it paranoia? – sink in. It could just be a tattoo, of course, but was she really willing to run that risk?

She looked back up at the man. He wasn't dressed like the men Sam had described at all - instead of the well-tailored suits he opted for a casual shirt and ripped jeans - but Alice was feeling distinctly uneasy. He certainly wasn't the same as the men she'd seen in the pub, but seeing that symbol had sent a frisson of fear running down her spine. If there was one thing she had learned, it was to trust her instincts.

'Sure,' she said after a short pause, leaning in a bit closer towards the man.

'What do you fancy?'

'Surprise me!'

The man walked off towards the bar, his gait strangely measured and completely asynchronous to the music blaring through the sound system.

She watched him walk away, and tried to get her thoughts straight. *Am I just being paranoid now too?* It was certainly possible, she wouldn't have thought much about a man offering her a drink on any other day, but she couldn't get the thought out of her head that something more sinister was at play. *Bloody Sam, can't have a normal life!*

When she was sure he wouldn't be able to see her, Alice quickly picked up her bag and made her way back towards the stairs of the club. She didn't have time to say to her friends that she was heading back home – even if she did, it might not be a good idea – she just wanted to disappear into the night and leave all this conspiracy paranoia behind. She snaked through throngs of people dancing, weaving her way as quickly as possible through the crowd and checking behind herself to make sure he wasn't following. He wasn't; he was still at the bar completely unaware that Alice was making a hasty escape.

Pharrell Williams' *Happy* came blaring through the sound system, and Alice quickly made her leave of the club.

The rain fell heavily on Islington that night, and the walk home was longer and darker than Alice had thought it would be. She kept checking over her shoulder, eyeing every passer-by with the utmost suspicion. Her mind raced with everything Sam had said. His fear, his paranoia. She understood it now. Thinking back, she remembered the man in the sleek black car who'd offered her a lift. Then she thought of the Men in

Black look-a-likes at the pub, exactly as Sam had described them, and with an unsettling vibe about them. And now the man in the club, with his tattoo so reminiscent of the Was sceptre. What if it was all in her head? Maybe Sam and James's talk of conspiracies was getting to her, and she was starting to see threats where there weren't any. She tried to talk herself out of the paranoid delusions, but Alice knew that something didn't feel right. She tried to listen to the voice of reason, but after everything she'd experienced that day, something told her what she didn't want to hear. Sam was right.

She walked up to the front door of her building and let herself in. It was deathly quiet inside and the lights were off, which hardly helped Alice with her sense of uneasiness. Closing the door behind her, she started making her way up the stairs to her second floor flat. She just couldn't wait to get into bed, get some rest and reassess things with a clearer head in the morning. Maybe Sam or James would know something else by the morning.

Keys jangled and her bag landed with a soft *thoomp* sound as Alice threw them both onto the sofa. She stripped her rain-soaked denim jacket off, flinging over one of the hooks by the door, and she started to undress as she headed towards her bedroom. Picking up a towel she'd left on her floor that morning, Alice quickly dried herself off with it before slumping down on the bed. She'd just closed her eyes and could feel herself sinking into the soft enveloping rolls of her duvet, when her phone jolted her awake. She eyed it suspiciously, and saw across the screen the words: Sam Hain is calling.

'Hello?' Alice said as she answered the call, sounding more confused than she intended to.

'Hello,' the voice of Sam Hain said, 'you okay?'

'Sam, it's almost one in the morning,' Alice replied, 'why're you calling? You hate phone calls!'

'I know,' he said bluntly. Whether he meant he knew it was almost one, or he knew he hated phone calls, Alice wasn't sure. 'I just wanted to check, uh, make sure everything was all right... Have you had any, y'know, 'incidents'?'

Alice knew what he meant, and for a moment she considered lying and telling him that she'd had an entirely uneventful evening. After all, neither Rachel, Chantelle or Jess would have been aware of what Alice had noticed. If she was only seeing these things because Sam had unintentionally put the thought of it in her head, then she was reading into things that didn't need any reading into. But she knew on some level that that wasn't the case.

'Yeah,' she said sombrely, 'yeah.'

'Me too,' Sam said. A silence hung on the phone line for a short while. 'What happened?'

'These two guys, exactly how you described them, turned up at the pub earlier. I don't know, I think they were watching me. They didn't order a pint or talk to anyone. They just kind of stood there.' She paused. 'You're right, though. There's definitely something off about them.'

'Yeah, sounds like them… Creepy, sinister-looking bastards, aren't they?'

'There was also a man driving near your place in the afternoon who offered me a lift home. I didn't think much of it at the time, but looking back something was strange about that too – no-one in London is friendly enough to offer a stranger a lift! And another offered to buy me a drink at the club. They were all exactly as you described them... Well, except for the guy in the club, but he had a tattoo which looked like the Wazz sceptre.'

'Was sceptre.'

'Whatever.'

'But nothing else?' Sam asked.

'No. Why?'

'Okay. You realise that drink was probably going to be-'

'Spiked? I don't know, I suppose it crossed my mind, I couldn't tell if I was just being paranoid. I left there as soon as I could.'

'Good. And you're home safe and sound now?' He sounded relieved.

'Yeah, I am,' Alice replied, 'how about you?'

There was another sizeable silence before Sam answered.

'I was followed again,' he eventually said, 'four of them, at least. And a black van, tinted windows, no license plate. I took them on a run around the houses and through the park. Took me bloody hours to lose them.' He sighed. 'Ruined my lasagna.'

'Right,' she said. She tried to think of something else to say, something probably a bit more reassuring or proactive, but nothing came to her. She couldn't get her head around the reality of the situation they found themselves in, it was just too mind-boggling. But their experiences couldn't be chalked up to something as simple as paranoia, no matter how many times Alice tried to convince herself that was all it was. The more she considered the reality of it all, the more futile their situation seemed. 'So what are we going to do? Any word from James?'

There was nothing but silence the other end of the line. She waited to hear if Sam would eventually say something, but she couldn't even hear him breathing now. She looked at her phone screen, and the call had abruptly ended.

'Hello?' Sam said into the silent telephone. 'Hell-ooo?' The landline crackled, and went dead. Nothing. Not even the dull hum of a dialing tone.

He put the phone's handset down on the base unit and furrowed his brow. What if something had happened to Alice? His stomach twisted with worry. A low growl of thunder rolled overhead, which relaxed Sam a little bit; the weather had probably knocked out the phone line. It didn't do much to put his mind at ease, but he could at least try to call Alice from his mobile or text her. The living room curtains briefly flashed with light. This was followed by another noise, a loud rhythmic knocking, which Sam thought was a very peculiar sound for thunder to make. The knocking came again, and reluctantly Sam made his way to the front door.

Peering through the door's viewer, Sam could see a man in a fluorescent jacket standing on the doorstep. He had a lanyard around his neck, and looked very unhappy to be there. He wondered why this man was knocking on his door at this time of night, and with trepidation, Sam slowly and cautiously opened his front door. He left the chain across the latch, allowing the door to only open a couple of inches, and he peered through the gap.

The rain was building into a torrent, and the skies rumbled ominously. The man on the doorstep was a very wet looking man. His fluorescent jacket sounded almost like it was crackling as raindrops fell and bounced off of it, and a plastic hood was pulled over his head.

'Phone line repairs,' the wet man said, 'seems to be an issue on your line.' He held up an ID, hanging around his neck on a lanyard, and Sam inspected it. The man was indeed a telephone engineer.

Sam stared at him with confusion and suspicion, and blinked incredulously several times before he eventually spoke. 'What?'

'I said-'

'No, I know what you said. Why are you knocking on my door at one o-bloody-clock in the morning?'

'Crossed signals at the exchange,' the telephone engineer explained, 'been working on the junction box a couple of houses down in this bleedin' weather. I noticed a fault on your line, and seein' as your lights're on, thought I'd fix the issue.' The man smiled at Sam, who simply stared morosely back at him.

'I have had an incredibly long day. If there's a fault with the landline, I'm sure it can wait until the morning. Thank you.' Sam nodded and offered a small wave through the gap in the door.

As he was about to push the door shut, he heard a noise which sounded uncannily like the telephone engineer saying 'oh screw this', shortly followed by a much clearer sound of a boot kicking the door. Hard. The latch and chain flew off of the front door as it burst inwards, and before Sam had a chance to make sense of what was going on he felt a sudden and sharp pain hit the side of his skull. Darkness quickly swam in around him as he lost consciousness.

CHAPTER III

The sound of a humming engine filled Sam's ears. The world was still shrouded in darkness, his eyelids too heavy for him to open them, and his head pulsed in agony. He tried to piece together what had happened, but he couldn't even begin to get his thoughts straight.

The next thing he became aware of was the sensation of leather pressed against his right cheek. It was warm, and he could feel it sticking to his skin. Lifting his head slightly, he peeled his cheek away from the leather and went to rub the side of his face, but discovered that his hands were firmly bound together behind his back.

There was a clinking noise, as if two glasses had been knocked together, and the sound of hushed conversation came from somewhere in front of him. Slowly struggling to peel his eyes open, Sam tried to gauge his surroundings.

He was greeted by the sight of the inside of a limousine. It was brightly lit by several small spotlights, and two rows of black leather seats ran up the full length of the limo, contrasting with the sparkling white marble floor and mirrored ceiling. At the far end, just behind the driver's area, was a polished chrome mini-bar. Sam found himself staring sideways down the length of the limo from the very back seat.

What on Earth is going on?

Immediately ahead of him, not too far from the mini-bar, Sam could see two men in suits sat opposite each other. They were mid-conversation, keeping their voices low as they sipped from slender flutes of champagne. As Sam's vision started to come back into focus properly, he was sure he recognised the two of them from the café that morning. He could sense there were another two men sat either side of him too.

'Looks like our friend's coming 'round,' said the man on the left. He was the stockier of the pair, with the receding hairline.

'Wakey-wakey, sleepy-head,' chimed the one on the right, who was the taller, more slender of the two.

Sam struggled to sit up, discovering his feet were bound together too, and managed to shift himself into an almost upright position. Neither of the two men, nor those either side of him, bothered to help. 'Were-um Ah?' Sam managed to slur, and he shook his head the minute he heard and felt the words tumble sloppily from his mouth.

The Men in Black stared at him vacantly.

'Where. Am. I?' Sam repeated, making sure he was articulating his words properly. His tongue felt like an old sponge.

'You're in a limo,' stated the man on the right.

He took another sip of his champagne.

Sam swallowed hard. His head was throbbing, and the world around him was still decidedly blurry, but he was determined to struggle through his mental fug. He wanted answers and, although he hadn't wanted to find out on their terms, now was as good a time as any. 'I can see I'm in a limo,' Sam hissed bitterly at the man, 'but why?'

'So we can have a little chat,' he replied. Sam stared at him as if to prompt him to continue talking, but the man took a casual sip from his champagne without another word.

'So, let me guess,' Sam said after several minutes of silence, 'Agent Smith? Agent Jones?'

The stocky man on the left looked up. 'Yup,' he gruffly replied.

'Well, which one?'

'I'm Smith, he's Jones,' the slender man said, gesturing to his compatriot sat opposite him.

'You sure we should be just giving him this intel?' Agent Jones said, leaning towards Agent Smith.

'They are only code names, agent. There's not much our guest can do in his current predicament, is there?'

'He still knew our code names somehow. Evidently he's more cunning and resourceful than they gave him credit for.'

'Actually, I'm not,' Sam interrupted, and both of the agents stared at him. 'Lucky guess, really.' He smiled a half-sheepish, half-wry smile, hoping he was maintaining a sense of bravado, concealing how he really felt. Internally, he was bricking it.

'So what do they want us to do with him now?' Jones asked Smith.

'We're to present their proposal to him. Nothing more. It's up to him whether he'll choose to comply with their suggestions.'

Sam shifted awkwardly in the seat. It was quite distracting having his limbs bound and unable to move properly. 'Um, hi, I am still here,' he said, leaning towards the two agents, 'who are these 'they' you keep mentioning? What do 'they' want with me?' He would have used air quotations, but his hands were still firmly tied behind his back. Probably for the best, really, he doubted they'd have appreciated him miming air quotations.

'*They* are our employers,' said Smith, intentionally vague.

Now that Sam's vision was almost completely back to normal, he was sure he could see the bulging outline of a gun beneath Agents Smith and Jones's suits. This did nothing to put his mind at ease. It no longer hurt quite as much to move around, so he turned to face the two men sat either side of him. He noticed the man on his left also wore an identical suit with matching gun-bulge. The man on his right, however, looked very different to the others, and more than a little familiar. He wore a bright fluorescent vest, and a telephone engineer's ID hung around his neck.

'You're not really a telephone engineer, are you?' Sam said to him.

'No,' replied the man who wasn't a telephone engineer.

'I apologise for our forceful methods,' Agent Smith started to say, leaning back in his seat, 'but you left us with very little choice.'

'What, I didn't like being stalked by secret agents, so you had to assault and kidnap me? I can see how you didn't have a choice...'

Agent Smith simply sipped his champagne, and sighed a luxurious sigh. 'It got you here though, didn't it? No need to thank us for the luxury.'

'Yeah, I appreciate the thought of abducting me in a limousine – very premium – but it would be nice if I wasn't all tied up. I'd quite like to feel my feet again.' Sam twisted his face into a sarcastic smile. When in doubt, or in mortal danger, always try to be charmingly sarcastic: that was his new motto. Even if he was still shaking inside.

'All in good time,' said Agent Smith with a smug smile creeping up his face.

'Thing is, Sam, you're a liability,' Agent Jones said. 'You, and your line of work.'

'My colleague is right. If you carry on the way you have been, we might need to get involved. And I can assure you, you really don't want us getting involved.' Agent Smith raised his glass to Sam, and in unison all four agents nodded.

'Listen, I've been conscious for – what, five, ten minutes? – and everything you've said so far has just been irritatingly and intentionally vague. I want answers. No, more than that, I demand some bloody answers.' Sam was quite impressed with himself. From where he sat, he sounded commanding, full of conviction, not a shadow of doubt in his heart. He hoped it seemed that way to the agents, too. 'Now, who are you people? MI-5? MI-6?'

All four agents suddenly burst into laughter. Sam looked around at them, confused. *What'd I say that was so funny?* He may not have been in on the joke, but he felt a little at ease that they were laughing at something. At least they had human emotions underneath those perfectly tailored suits and calculated facial expressions.

'No, no. We'd never affiliate ourselves with those idiots,' Agent Smith said, his face slightly pink from laughter.

'You'd never catch one of us leaving confidential documents on a train!' Agent Jones exclaimed, and they all started laughing again.

'Let's just say that our employers are decidedly more... in control of things,' Agent Smith twirled his hand around as he explained. 'You see, our interests and yours aren't all that dissimilar, Sam. All we ask for is a little cooperation, to allow us to get on with our work uninterrupted.'

'Carry on as you are, though,' Jones interjected, 'and you'll only get in our way. Neither of us wants that now, do we?'

Sam stayed silent this time. He simply stared back at the two of them waiting for them to continue. Asking questions would clearly get him nowhere.

'Your little fiasco in Grimditch really

interrupted a project of ours,' Agent Smith said.

'Aha,' Sam said almost a little too triumphantly, 'so you *are* the Regents?'

'No, we are not the Regents,' said Agent Jones, 'we simply work for them.'

'And you say I got in the way of your project in Grimditch?' Sam scoffed. 'What I saw was the beginning of a situation which could easily have spiralled out of control into a god-damn bloodbath! I think our interests lie in very different directions if that was one of your 'projects'...'

'Rogue agents,' Agent Smith replied with a dismissive wave of the hand and an almost too nonchalant attitude, 'they took an artefact from the vaults and used it for their own purposes. To say they had it coming, well...' He raised his hands in a 'what can ya do?' kind of gesture.

'Why permit them to continue, then? Why did I get in the way if these men had gone rogue?'

'The Regents were intrigued,' Agent Smith said with glee, 'it's not every day one can observe a Class V Animating Possessor uninhibited.'

'The Pig-Headed Demon?' Sam clarified.

'Yes, as you oh-so eloquently put it, the Pig-Headed Demon.'

'We were ordered to allow the AP to continue without obstruction until its actions posed a legitimate threat,' Agent Jones added. 'You brought an untimely end to what was panning out to be a very promising project.'

'You don't think those men losing their lives and a demon possessing one of the corpses posed a threat?' Sam lowered his voice. Any sense of fear or paranoia had left him, most likely due to his righteous indignation and the sudden surge of adrenaline running through his veins. 'If you think what was happening there, what was going to continue happening there, was acceptable, then I'm afraid you are sorely mistaken. You didn't see what it was like. I saw the bodies, I saw the look on Douglas's ex-wife's face when she heard of his death, I saw that *thing* using people as its grotesque meat-puppets. Someone had to bring it to an end.'

'Don't try to be too sanctimonious about it, Sam. We knew about everything that was going on; we were there, observing events from the ground level,' Agent Smith said. That was when something clicked in Sam's memory, and he stared at Smith for a moment. As his eyes focused on Smith's face, he knew he recognised it from somewhere.

'I thought you seemed familiar, *Officer* Smith,' Sam said, and internally he kicked himself for not recognising the principle police officer who had been on every scene in the Grimditch case.

'Same alias, same face, different uniform,' Agent Smith nodded in confirmation. 'Playing the part of such a prosaic pedestrian plod felt like a bit of a demotion, but the Regents were insistent I was there to oversee the unfolding of events. Our involvement had to be entirely unobtrusive, unremarkable, so as not to influence the course of events or the intelligence we gathered, and were prepared to pull the plug on the whole operation when necessary.'

'Human lives were lost!' Sam exclaimed. His righteous frustration was now behind the steering wheel, while his anxiety was sat by the side of it trying to reign it in a bit, desperately hoping he didn't antagonise them too much.

'The men who lost their lives were expendable. They turned their backs on the Regents and tried to pursue research into that artefact - and that entity - on their own, for their own purposes. We could've stopped them from the start, but we allowed them to continue, and in exchange we got a hint of the results we were hoping for. Witnessing what that Class V was capable of was fascinating. You should consider it a miracle that the whole situation was as tame as it was.' Agent Smith quaffed the last of his champagne. Sam held his tongue.

'We want the same thing as you,' said Agent Jones, adopting an almost gentle tone, 'to keep the people of this world safe. For thousands of years, the Regents have been the guardians of arcane knowledge on Earth; and we've been there to keep the praeternatural world under wraps, under control. But to do that, we need to better understand the forces we're dealing with. Harnessing the power of the Akashic field; interdimensional travel; the quarantine, containment, and elimination of demonic threats. These pursuits naturally come with great risks, but they are risks which must be taken. Surely you've seen the signs yourself, whispers from the void that a darkness is coming… We need to be prepared.'

'All we're asking is that you take a step back. Stop prying into our organisation, and stop interfering in paranormal events with little regard for what we could achieve if we see them through to the end. All we need is that things remain as they are, and upstarts such as yourself stay out of our way.' Agent Smith had suddenly taken on a menacing tone, and he glared at Sam, his eyes seemingly burning into him.

'Right,' Sam said, 'we'll just have to agree to disagree then.' He swallowed hard, and felt his heart sink into his stomach as he dared to stand his ground. *Will they kill me for this?* 'I will not sit idly by while innocent lives are at risk, or when something from beyond this world needs to be dealt with. You carry on with your 'experiments', I'll still do everything in my power to protect the ordinary from the extraordinary.' He was kind of proud of that last sentence, and in a brief moment of whimsy he considered it being his new slogan.

'I had hoped you'd listen to reason. Very well, never mind,' Agent Smith said coldly, and he casually gave a quick flick of his hand. Sam felt a sharp pain in the back of his head again, and his world was once again engulfed in darkness.

CHAPTER IV

Alice awoke early the next morning with a troubled mind. Not with the hangover she'd expected to have, but with worry. She'd been trying to call Sam back ever since the phones had cut out, but his landline was off the hook, and he didn't answer his mobile. She text him, but he hadn't replied. It wasn't unusual for him to be difficult to contact, but something about this occasion made Alice's stomach uneasy, especially after their conversation the day before. Something didn't feel right.

She had tried to talk to Rachel about Sam's sudden disappearance, either for help in reaching him or for reassurance that he'd be okay, she didn't know. Rachel had not been much help.

'Is 'e your new lover?' She had slurred in the early hours of the morning when she came stumbling in from the club.

'It's nothing like that,' Alice had tried to say, but Rachel continued to tease her.

'*Alice and Sam, sittin' in a tree-*' Rachel chimed in an irritatingly sing-song voice. She could probably have tolerated her if she'd been drunk too, but when sober Alice found Rachel to be an incredibly annoying drunk. She'd decided to leave Rachel to it at that point, and went to bed. Sleep did not come easily for her that night, as she lay awake with conspiracies running riot in her mind. When she did eventually succumb to sleep, her consciousness slowly drifted into that place somewhere between wakefulness and dreaming. In these waking-dreams, she saw Sam being taken by the Men in Black, bound and tied and in the back of a car, being taken to some sinister underground chamber.

She hoped Sam would be in contact in the morning. She hoped to wake up to find a message saying: 'Sorry, drifted off,' or 'Sorry I couldn't call you back, but...'

Alice woke up to find no such message. She was worried. Thankfully, Rachel was in a much more sedate mood that morning, but she was still just as unhelpful.

'I think I remember you mentioning him last night... New boyfriend?' She'd said with a wry smile.

'No, I said last night it was nothing like that.'

'Oh. So why are you worried? Men will only message you when it suits them, especially if they know there's no chance for anything else. He'll be in touch when he wants to,' Rachel said, as if she was imparting sagely advice. There was a momentary pause while she squeezed her eyes tight and put her hand to her forehead. 'Ugh, my head! I had *so* much to drink last night.'

'He disappeared in the middle of a call last

night. He wouldn't just hang-up without saying goodbye or without sending a message, he's not like that,' Alice replied, ignoring Rachel's traditional drinking boasts. 'What if something's happened?'

'Like what?' Rachel asked. Her motionless face showed she didn't really want to know, and was more preoccupied with her hangover-induced self-pity.

'I don't know, I just have a bad feeling,' Alice said, thinking of all the things which could have happened but would sound far too insane to say out loud. *Secret agents, conspiracies, assassinated, abducted*, she thought, *attacked by a demon, possessed...*

'You really need to relax, everything's bound to be fine. 'Bad feelings' often don't mean anything,' Rachel said. She craned her neck around to look towards the kitchen. 'I don't suppose you're thinking of brewing a pot of coffee, are you?'

'I'll stick the kettle on then, shall I?' Alice said, making her way towards the kitchen. *If you'd seen the things I'd seen*, she thought, *you wouldn't say that bad feelings don't mean anything.*

After having a couple of cups of coffee – the strength of which gave Alice a caffeine high and coffee shakes, and restored some life to Rachel's hangover-face – Alice quickly ate a cereal bar and got dressed. She wasn't hanging around any longer waiting for Sam to get in touch, she had to go and make sure he was okay.

'I'm going to meet the others for a nice greasy breakfast at the café around the corner, if you want to come with us?' Rachel had offered when she saw Alice slip into her dress and throw a jacket around her shoulders. She politely said no, and made her excuses before leaving. She wasn't going to tell Rachel that she was going to Sam's house to check on him; she'd only say she was making a big deal out of nothing. She didn't particularly want to be grilled on her relationship with him when things were already mad and difficult enough to explain.

Alice arrived at the house on Constantine Road around mid-morning, clutching her jacket around her. The cold wind was particularly biting that morning. The streets were darkened by the rainfall the night before, and puddles of water gleamed and reflected the grey skies above like murky mirrors.

Sam's house seemed eerie and imposing in the weird, greyish-white light of the day, but there was something else which really put Alice on edge. As she approached the house, she saw that the door was ajar. Tentatively pushing the door open, Alice took a cautious step into the hallway. 'Hello?' She called out, but no-one answered. The house felt eerily deserted. Heading towards the stairs down to Sam's flat, Alice peered in the rooms which lead off from the hallway, but there was no sign that anybody was home; neither Sam or his landlady.

Her footsteps echoed and the floorboards creaked as she cautiously made her way downstairs. The door to Sam Hain's basement flat was shut, but as she tried the handle, Alice discovered it was unlocked. Gently pushing the door open, she stepped inside and peered tentatively into the room. Immediately Alice noticed something was amiss. Sam's coat and hat were still hung up on the antique coat stand. At first she guessed he must have left in a hurry, but she knew him better than that: he would never leave his hat and coat behind, not even in an emergency.

The house felt hauntingly empty. As she took a few more steps into Sam's living room, Alice felt like the hairs on the back of her neck were standing on end. An unnerving feeling tingled at the back of her mind. 'Sam? You there?' She called out again, but already knew she'd receive no answer.

Her dream from the night before flashed through her mind. Visions of Sam being taken by the Men in Black, bundled into a car and taken to an underground lair. She started to wonder if it had really been just a dream, or something else, something more. *What do I do?* She paced, lost in her thoughts. *What can I...? How...?*

'You can start by trusting in your particular talents,' a voice came from behind her. Alice jumped and whirled around, only to see James Mortimer standing in the doorway. Despite his slender build, James seemed to take up the whole of the doorway.

'How did you...? What're you doing here? Where's Sam?' Alice asked in a barrage of questions as her thoughts all attempted to jostle to the forefront.

'Same as you,' James said, stepping into the room and sitting down on the sofa. 'I don't know what's happened or where Sam is, but something is very wrong.' He gestured to the hat and coat hung up, Sam-less and abandoned. 'I figured I'd find you here, though. You're one of the few who'd know something was amiss.'

Alice nodded uncertainly. She went to sit in the armchair, but hesitated and hovered by the side of it for a while. Nervous energy compelled Alice to stay standing. Too many thoughts were running through her head all at once, and pacing around the room seemed like something someone with too many thoughts would do. 'He suddenly cut out on the phone last night, and I haven't been able to contact him since. You don't think-?'

'That he was right?' James stretched his arms, and clasped his hands together behind his head, leaning back against one of the mismatched throw pillows. 'I don't know. I've known Sam a long time, and he's been right about even stranger things before. This,' he said, gesturing around the room and its conspicuous lack of Sam Hain, 'I'd say at least suggests he wasn't wrong.'

'Yeah. Definitely,' Alice said, sounding almost distant as she spoke. 'They came for me too, last night. The Men in Black. At least, I think they did, I'm not sure. I might've just been imagining things, but... No. I don't think I was.'

James leaned forward. 'What happened?'

Alice recounted the events of the night before. She told James everything that had happened, from the seemingly otherworldly men in well-tailored suits - exactly as Sam had described them - at the pub to the Was sceptre tattoo on the clubber who offered her a drink. The more she looked back, the more it began to dawn on Alice that had it not been for Sam talking about conspiracies and the Men in Black that day, these would have been wholly unremarkable events. But there was more to it than that; the sense of fear and dread Alice had felt wasn't just conjured up by seeing two men in black suits. There was a distinct presence to them, an otherness which she couldn't quite put her finger on. Whatever it was, they gave off an aura which had made Alice feel uneasy.

James listened to her tale intently, but whether any of it surprised him or evoked any thoughts or feelings at all was impossible to tell. His face was unchanging, sat with the same neutral expression, and Alice started to wonder if he was even listening. She finished recalling the previous night, adding that had it not been for Sam's ranting, she might have disappeared exactly as he had.

'That's good,' James said, and when Alice shot him a strange look he added, 'that you had your wits about you. It'd be easy for you to overlook them and carry on as normal - anything for a quiet life - either dismissing it as needless paranoia or not even noticing anything is wrong at all. But you had the acuity to know something was up. That's a vital skill to have, especially when Sam Hain is a part of your life.'

'There's also… No, that's not important,' Alice started, but stopped herself mid-sentence. She thought it best to leave the story with only the solid facts. 'The point is, our phone call suddenly cut out, and since then I haven't been able to reach Sam at all.'

'Alice, if there's one thing I've learned, it's that there's nothing that's not important. Everything is interconnected in one way or another, whether we realise it or not,' James said, and Alice could almost hear Sam's voice echoing those words. 'What was it?'

Alice waved her hand dismissively. 'It was just a dream. I didn't sleep well last night, but I had one of those half-asleep dreams that Sam had been tied up by the Men in Black and shoved in the back of a limousine. They were taking him to some kind of supervillain lair underground. After everything else, it was probably just all of the built-up stress.'

'On the contrary,' James stood up, 'Sam told me you were a latent psychic, and I see what he means now. You probably don't even realise it yourself half of the time.'

'I'm not entirely sure I realise it now, to be honest.'

'Hypnagogic clairvoyance.'

'Hypnagogic clairvoyance?' Alice echoed.

'It's like having a vision during the transitional state between wakefulness and sleep. Those strangely vivid dreams, especially when you're half-asleep, which you can't shake the feeling were somehow quite profound, even if they didn't make much sense.'

'Dreams, basically.'

'It's no secret that dreams can give you some insight into your life, even if it isn't apparent at first. Some dreams can show you something more, though.'

'So you're saying you think that that was more than just a bad night's sleep, and I somehow managed to remote-view Sam being abducted,' Alice said, and her tone was laced with scepticism.

'It's a theory. It's worth looking into, at least. Can you remember any specific details? Any idea where they went to get to this underground lair?'

Alice shook her head. She could only recall the dream in brief flashes. Sam was tied up in the back of a limo, surrounded by Men in Black, and taken somewhere which put Alice in mind of old wartime bunkers. There was nothing which particularly stood out as a clear and distinct detail, and she forced herself to remember more of the dream. Try as she might, the dream fragments refused to give up any more information. 'I'm sorry,' was all she could say.

Running his hand through his hair, James slowly wandered over to the window. There wasn't much to see out of it, mostly just the sight of a wall, but the very top of the window could just about see the street level, which allowed for a small amount of natural light. He gazed up and out through the small space, to the white-grey skies beyond. He felt like they should have had something more to go on, but instead they were now missing one detective. There was only one thing left which, although it wasn't his favourite idea, might help them get that bit closer.

'You remember I mentioned that conspiracy theorist yesterday?' James said, his gaze still focussed outside the window.

'The escapee test subject? Yeah, I do…'

'I'm going to reach out to him, see if he's willing to share the information he claims to have. You never know,' he said, turning around to face Alice, 'if his intel's genuine, he might be able to shed some light on what you saw in your dream.'

'And if he doesn't agree?' Alice almost hated the tone of her question, but she was feeling more than helpless. Everything seemed so futile in that moment, pessimism came easily. It clearly gave James pause for thought too, as he stared at the floor in silent contemplation for a moment.

'Then we keep on digging until we strike gold,' he said, 'but we'll worry about that if this doesn't pan out. While I make contact, you need to keep a low profile until we know more. We can't risk anything happening to you too.' When he noticed the worried look in Alice's eyes, James quickly added, 'not that anything will happen to you.'

Strangely, this didn't do much to assuage Alice's worries.

James had insisted he give Alice a lift back to Islington. Even though he had stressed he didn't feel she was in any immediate danger, he thought it was best to err on the side of caution. She had agreed. The events of the night before had unnerved her to say the least, and with Sam now nowhere to be found, Alice felt even less secure. If they could take Sam from his own home, where was safe?

The drive back to Islington was a short one. The traffic had been very forgiving, and Alice was back home within quarter of an hour. She and James had sat in awkward silence for most of the journey, occasionally trying to make idle small talk to fill the time, but they both had their minds set on bigger things. It was hard to focus on anything else. Alice kept probing her memory for more snippets from the dream, anything which might give them some kind of answer.

Nothing new came to her. Only an uneasy feeling which twisted and turned in the pit of her stomach.

That afternoon, Alice stayed at home. Partially because of James suggesting she keep a low profile, but also because leaving the house felt like an insurmountable challenge. Instead, she tried to unwind as much as she could given the circumstances, but that was another challenge in and of itself. She had picked up a book and tried to read and relax, but she couldn't get into it. Her mind kept wandering to the Regents, the Men in Black, and Sam Hain. She lay on the sofa, flicking through the TV channels to find something she could lose herself in. There wasn't much on, but she watched one of the afternoon films. It was nothing more than a bit of light entertainment, but she felt like it was what she needed to calm her nerves; which it did, for an hour and a half. When the credits began to roll, the fear and uncertainty crept their way back in.

No matter what she tried to do, she couldn't shut off from everything that was going on. She was a mess of nerves, but outwardly all she could express was a quiet and despondent moodiness.

Rachel, thankfully, didn't try to pry into her friend's moody state, and instead allowed her her personal space, except to bring her a cup of tea and a family-size bar of chocolate for emotional support. Alice smiled a thank-you, but as much as she appreciated the gesture, it was going to take more than tea and chocolate to fix this particular situation. Not that that stopped her from enjoying the whole bar.

It wasn't until early that evening that she began to feel like things may be starting to look up. James had text her, and the seeds of a plan were beginning to grow.

Chapter V

The conspiracy theorist had agreed to share what he knew with James, on one condition: the conversation would have to be conducted in person. He didn't trust most forms of communication, believing they were being monitored, and rathered they met face-to-face to discuss things. The man had introduced himself through a message as Cypher, followed shortly by another message which mentioned a Caesar salad and a string of seemingly random letters: *zrrg ng ternfl fcbba pnss rqtjner.*

James was no stranger to deciphering encoded messages, and he had made short work of this one. It was vague, but it was simple enough to point James in the right direction, and he set out to meet Cypher immediately.

The Greasy Spoon Café, as was its name, was a fairly dingy affair. On a street somewhere in North London, surrounded by independent taxi companies, corner shops and a launderette, the Greasy Spoon lived up to its name. An old and weathered sign - which looked as basic as the café itself - stretched across the front of the café, and large windows covered the entire street-facing wall. In the windows, the Greasy Spoon boasted a few of its menu options, including 'All-Day English Breakfast' and 'Coffee'.

The sound of a small bell chimed as James pushed the door open and stepped inside. The four other occupants of the café stopped what they were doing and stared at James with suspicion. Sat in the corner, a grizzled old man with a long beard and tired eyes peered over the top of his newspaper, and then resumed reading. Two men, both wearing orange hi-vis jackets and dusty overalls, briefly stopped eating their fry-ups to look up. Towards the back of the café, a bald, weathered-looking man in an old army coat was hunched over a steaming cup of coffee. He didn't look up, but he shifted nervously in his seat. *He must be the guy*, James thought.

He started to make his way towards the back of the café. Stood behind the counter, a friendly-faced man in grease-stained chef whites smiled at James as he walked past. James felt like he was overdressed for this kind of place, his pristine grey suit clashing with the off-white floor and stained wooden tables. Nonetheless, he nodded to the man behind the counter and with a wave he simply said, 'coffee, black.'

'Right you are, guv. Cup o' worm dirt, comin' up,' replied the server.

James slid himself into the seat opposite the man in the army coat, who made very little effort to greet him. 'Are you the man they call Cypher?'

The question caught the man's attention, and

his head snapped up to face James. His eyes were manic and bloodshot, and they darted back and forth as if he was having difficulty choosing where to focus his gaze. 'Who's asking?' He asked aggressively.

'I'll take that as a 'yes,' then,' James said with a smile, and he extended his hand. 'Mortimer. James Mortimer.' The man who went by the name of Cypher ignored James's hand, and instead stared at him with wary eyes.

'You're that chap who wanted to talk about *them*,' Cypher said, and when James nodded he added, 'mad bastard.'

'Here you are, friend, your wakey-wakey juice. That'll be two squid,' the server announced with a warm smile, placing a large white cup in front of James. It was filled to the brim with a steaming black liquid which looked more like oil than coffee, and from certain angles it even had the same opalescent shimmer as oil.

James gave the server a cursory 'thank you' as he handed him a two pound coin. He took a sip of the coffee, only to discover that it had very little taste to it. It simply tasted of scolding hot water and a bitter earthiness. *Worm dirt indeed,* James mused as he stared into his cup. All the while, Cypher kept his gaze on James as if he was analysing his every move.

'Now,' James said, looking up from his disappointing coffee, 'it seems our meeting couldn't have come a moment too soon. Yes, I want to talk about *them*. I've read over a couple of your leaks, but I'm hoping your unique insight can help me with something.'

'No one wants help from a crazy old coot like me,' Cypher said derisively, not taking his eyes off of James. Something about the wild but distant look in his eyes told James that this man was not all-there in the traditional sense, but there was still a keen mind ticking away somewhere inside the paranoia-twisted psyche. With a pained chuckle, Cypher took a gulp from his own coffee cup. 'Here to finish me, is it?'

'I'm sorry?'

'Put me outta my misery, silence my gob for good,' Cypher continued, his unbreaking and unblinking stare still fixed on James. 'Make it look like I topped myself, am I right? Crazy ol' conspiracy nut couldn't take his paranoia no more, decided to end it all.'

James stared at him with a mixture of confusion and disbelief. He'd expected his meeting with Cypher to be an unusual one, but he wasn't quite expecting this. 'I think you misunderstand me, I'm-'

'You're not fooling me,' Cypher interrupted, 'I've had more dealings with your kind than I can count. Your games won't work with me. I know what you are.' Without warning, Cypher grabbed James's hand and in a single swift and remarkably precise motion he stabbed a knife into James's palm and cut along the soft flesh. James yelped in pain and forcefully pulled his hand back from the lunatic, instinctively reaching for a napkin and holding it against his unexpected wound.

'What the?! Jesus! What the hell was that for, you maniac?!' James exclaimed. Several of the other café patrons looked up to see what the commotion was about, but almost instantly decided to turn a blind eye and not get involved.

His body surged with pain and anger as the shock subsided. Droplets of deep red blood dripped onto the table, and he had to press the napkin firmly against the cut across his palm to stem the bleeding. The formerly white napkin started to turn crimson. Cypher stared in disbelief. 'For Christ's sake, man, you look like you've never seen blood before,' James spat.

'I... I-I'm sorry,' Cypher stuttered, suddenly looking confused and frightened. He was transfixed by James's bleeding hand, gazing at the blood in disbelief. 'I thought- I didn't think...'

'You didn't think what?' James's eyes seemed to turn black as he glared at his unexpected assailant.

'I didn't think you'd bleed.'

'Well what the shit did you think was going to happen?!'

Cypher continued to stare, but he was no longer looking at James or the freshly drawn blood. He looked like his mind was no longer in the café with them, as if his consciousness had mentally checked out and retreated to the back of his mind. 'You're real. You're... human?'

James nodded a slow and sarcastic nod. 'Yes... I'm human. Were you expecting someone else?'

'I thought you were one of, you know… *Them*.'

'The Men in Black?'

'You look like they do. All prim and proper in their pretentious suits,' Cypher replied, and he seemed to spit his words with venom. He suddenly snapped out of his distant stare, and looked up at James. 'Thing is,' he said, leaning forward and lowering his voice to a conspiratorial whisper, '*they* don't bleed.'

'What do you mean?'

'I mean exactly how it bloody sounds. Prick us, do we not bleed? Because they sodding well don't. Listen, I've been runnin' from those creepy sons of bitches for years now, always havin' to watch my back. Can't trust no-one these days.' He leaned back into his seat and took the last swig of his coffee. He was notably more sane-looking than a moment ago (benefited by the fact that he was no longer wielding a knife), even if his words were still barbed and bilious. 'When you strode in all tall 'n' toffee-nosed, I pegged you as one o' them. I wasn't just gonna bolt out the door, see, that plays into their hands.'

James looked down at his own hand as Cypher babbled on. Thankfully the knife hadn't cut deep, and although it was absolute agony, the napkin was managing to stem the bleeding. He adjusted his grip on his hand, and quickly applied a clean napkin to the wound.

'Now, when you're confronted by somethin', what do you do? You got two choices; fight, or flight, innit? So I was always runnin', hidin', until one day they had me cornered. Only two of 'em, and way I saw it, I could take 'em. I couldn't run, so figured I'd at least go down swingin'. So I pulled me pen knife on them, and when one of the bastards tried to get too close, I stabbed 'im!' The table jolted as Cypher mimed himself stabbing an invisible agent. Repeatedly, with slightly more passion than telling the story really warranted, and certainly more than James was comfortable with. 'But me knife just came back out, clean as anything. No blood on the blade, or on their poncey easy-iron shirts, not even a reaction as you might expect from someone who's got a knife in their gut. So sorry I cut you up some, I really wasn't expectin' you to be an actual person.'

For a madman, Cypher seemed genuinely apologetic about stabbing James in the hand. If it weren't for the still searing pain in his palm, James would almost have considered putting the whole event behind them. As it happened, he wasn't even in the mood to say something to vaguely accept the apology. 'If you can't hurt them, then how did you escape?'

'Well I fuggin' twatted 'em, didn't I?' Cypher replied with a triumphant laugh. 'They might not bleed and you might not be able to kill 'em, but you can still stun 'em with a swift punch in the face. They might look it, but those Men in Black ain't exactly what you'd call human.'

'What would you call them, then?' James asked, intrigued. His hand had started to throb, and he wrapped it around his coffee mug, hoping that the heat would help to quell the pain. 'If,' he added, 'you trust me more since cutting my hand open?'

'They're creatures born out of necessity. The Regents needed people to do their dirty work for 'em, see? But people-people, like me 'n' you, we have flaws. We have emotions, consciences. We crack under pressure, we feel pain, we-'

'Bleed?' James interrupted snarkily, and he gave Cypher a wry smile.

'Yeah. Basically, we cock up and are kind of crap sometimes. To err is human, after all. And there are quite a few in the organisation that are human, but them Regents don't want no mortal screwin' up their wet work and accidentally lettin' things slip. Not when it comes to the real important stuff. That's where these Men in Black come in. They have these creepy automaton buggers do their biddin' for 'em, like little worker bees. Buzz buzz buzz.' Cypher traced patterns in the air with his fingers as he continued to make buzzing noises. 'Drones to serve the Hive. They can buzz off for all I care!'

'I must admit, your story intrigues me, Cypher. You've had far more experience dealing with them than I have,' James said, trying to ignore Cypher's occasional buzzing noise. Through what could be seen as the ramblings of a lunatic, James felt like he was getting somewhere. 'Do you know what they are, precisely? These Men in Black drones?'

Cypher could only offer a shrug in response. 'Beats me. All I know is they ain't exactly from this particular terrestrial plane of existence, if you catch me drift. Upset the Hive and they'll come and sting ya. Trust me, you don't wanna get stung by them.'

'So I gather. I can't say I've had any encounters with them myself, and the more I'm learning about them the happier I am about that. In fact, I knew next to nothing about the Regents until I read your leaks.' James swilled the coffee around his mug thoughtfully.

'I ain't surprised you never heard of 'em before. Not many have, they make sure of that. The Regents pull all the strings from behind the curtain, and if one of their little puppets don't dance right, then...' He drew his finger across his throat and grimaced to drive home his point.

'And you got away from them alive?'

'Obviously. I'm 'ere ain't I?'

James shook his head and made a noise that was somewhere between a laugh and an exasperated sigh. 'I mean, how did you escape from the Hive without getting... stung?'

'Ah. I just been lucky, I guess. Every few months I 'ave a bit of a ding-dong with their chaps in black. They try to take me back, and I give 'em the slip. Ain't no force in Heaven or Hell going take me back there.' And Cypher was gone again, his focus slipped away and he stared at nothing in particular with a far off gaze.

'Hey, are you still with me Cypher?'

'Yeah, mate, yeah,' Cypher said, suddenly snapping back to reality. 'Sorry, Voidwalker side-effects. Reality ain't quite what it seems when you been through that.'

'Through what, precisely?' James asked, leaning across the table. 'What was the Voidwalker Project?'

'Mad bastards,' Cypher replied and he shook his head. 'Somethin' to do with extra-dimensional research, portals to other realities, that kind of thing. People like ol' muggins here were their little guinea pigs. Sending us through their portals, using magic nodes to send our minds astral travellin', see if we didn't come back with our psyche's snapped in half. I've seen all kinds of mad shit. I've seen that void between worlds, that infernal howlin' abyss. And them words, echoin' across that void, that some kinda darkness is comin'. It ain't right.'

'And you got away from that intact? It's incredible you're still here to tell the tale.' James had more than a hunch that maybe Cypher's mind hadn't quite made it back from its extra-dimensional travels in one piece. But if Cypher had managed to break free from one of their facilities and been able to evade the Regents and the Men in Black for so long, he clearly still had his wits about him. He seemed cognizant enough to be of some use in helping Sam Hain.

'You don't need to patronise me, friend,' Cypher said solemnly, 'I know I ain't all there in the 'ead no more. Can't odds that when you're made to hop across alternate dimensional realities, like a mouse runnin' around a maze in some lab. I still got me wits and me mind, it's just them signals between mind and brain that have gone a bit skew-whiff.'

'I'm sorry, I didn't mean for it to sound like that. There's no doubt you've still got a firm grasp of your wits; you managed to break free from their facility, and have stayed ahead of their game, avoiding capture or worse.' James sounded genuinely impressed. It must be no mean feat evading the Men in Black - especially if it was true, as Cypher said, that they weren't human - let alone escaping from the Regents' facility. If they held enough sway to manifest their own unnatural operatives, and were powerful enough to conduct things like the Voidwalker project, he couldn't imagine breaking out was a walk in the park. 'So how did you escape? It can't have been easy.'

Cypher stared into his now empty coffee cup morosely, and stayed silent. After a while, he looked up again. 'No, it wasn't.' His words were clear and simple, and it was probably the sanest, or most serious, his voice had sounded all morning. 'I was bein' held in one of their detention facilities. When they wasn't sendin' us into hell, they kept us locked up below ground. Nothin' much to say about that hovel, just some concrete bunker for their little lab rats and worse. The ones who had already lost their minds were the lucky ones, blissfully deluded, least they weren't aware they was stuck in some concrete cell day-in day-out.

'One day - I dunno when precisely, time is an immaterial construct we perceive to make sense of our linear reality, but it's a fair bit more fiddly than that - anyway, one day, this alarm starts goin' off. *Bweee-ooo! Bweee-ooo!* And I kinda twig, 'hullo, somethin's goin' on here.' So I press my 'ead against the door and see if I can hear anything. Course, I can't hear a chuffin' thing, cells are soundproof 'cept for the alarms. Then, the door begins to shake, see, and the sound of the lock being opened. Door swings open, and there's this chap in an 'ospital gown with wires comin' outta 'is head. Another Voidwalker.

'Well I didn't waste no time, I joined the blighter and ran. Turns out there'd been some kinda containment breach, something had come back with my escapee friend and them agents were scramblin' to send the bloody thing back.'

'What was it?' James interrupted. He was getting impatient, and he was desperate to get to some information which might be useful in finding and rescuing Sam. *Still*, he thought to himself, *Cypher's intel is certainly informative.*

'You think I hung around to find out what all the excitement was about? Bollocks to that! I ran. There's only a handful of agents in that place, so most of 'em were busy tryin' to stop a transdimensional incursion while we made a break for it. One of 'em spotted us, and tezzered my pal, but I managed to stay hidden. I was lucky enough to get out. Had to keep all stealthy-like, obviously, didn't want no other suit spottin' me. When I got topside, I found meself in that royal park. Regent's Park, that's the one. Nice place when the weather's good.'

'Regent's Park?' James repeated, almost incredulously. 'The underground facility you escaped from was beneath Regent's Park?'

'Yeah, funny that. You'd think they'd name it somethin' less conspicuous.'

'So if you got out, you'd know how to find the way back in?'

'Why the titty-lovin' Christ would you want to know how to get in?'

'One of my friends, well, my oldest friend, believed he was being followed by the Men in Black yesterday. I've known him long enough now to know he wasn't just being paranoid. It turns out he was involved in a situation that was connected with the Regents-'

'Oof, nasty stuff.'

'And this morning, he's nowhere to be found. His flat is empty, and he suddenly dropped out of contact late last night. There's no doubt in my mind that what he feared would happen, has happened,' James said, his voice betraying his concern.

'Then they've probably taken him to the Hub,' Cypher said, and his face contorted apologetically. 'Your friend ain't comin' back out.'

James slammed his fist on the table, and instantly regretted it as pain seared from the wound in his hand. He'd been so distracted by coming close to a revelation that he'd almost forgotten that this man had greeted him by stabbing his hand. Wincing, he pulled his hand back slowly and gently nursed it under the table. 'That's not good enough,' he said, his voice mixed with anger, pain and desperation, 'you got out in one piece, even if your mind didn't. There must be a way.'

'Very different kettle of fish. There was some kind of hellbeast clawing its way out of the abyss, the Men in Black were distracted! Barring another monster attack, they won't be so easy to get by. It'd be suicide.'

'Just tell me how to get to this Hub. I'll worry about whether it's suicide or not.'

Cypher stared at the table for what felt like an eternity, and he'd murmur incoherently to himself every now and again, as if he was debating whether he would help or not. He felt sorry for James's situation, and for what had happened to his friend, but he wasn't sure he could burden the guilt of sending someone to their doom. No matter how well-intentioned. But then an idea struck him, a terrible idea which stoked a fire in his heart, and a darkly satisfied smile crept across his face.

'One condition,' he said, 'I come with you.'

'Don't be absurd! You just said it would be suicide.'

'The only life I can remember was either spent in their dingy little cells, or runnin' from their creepy goons. I got nothin' to lose. If you pull this off - and I jus' reckon you might, you crazy git - then I can get some of me own back.' Something glimmered in Cypher's eye, a kind of maniacal glee which unnerved James slightly. But maybe someone who already knew about the facility, someone who was knowledgeable if more than a little unhinged and fueled with revenge, was exactly who they needed.

James extended his non-cut hand towards Cypher. This time around, he took it and shook his hand firmly. 'Okay, you have a deal,' James said, 'but first and foremost, this is a search and rescue operation. There will be no heroics, no unnecessary risks. Understood?'

'Yes, boss!' Cypher exclaimed and gave him a wonky salute. 'Meet me in the north-west corner of Regent's Park, ten-a-clock tonight. I'll take ya to the Hub and into the mouth of hell. We'll get your buddy out.'

'Thank you,' James said, and he was hit by a wave of relief now that things were moving forwards. He had the man with inside knowledge on their side and by tomorrow morning, he told himself, Sam Hain would be safe and sound. Then he was hit by a wave of anxiety when the reality of infiltrating a secret organisation sunk in, but he tried not to think about it.

Standing up from the table, James returned his coffee mug to the counter of The Greasy Spoon, for which the server thanked him, and he turned to face his unusual co-conspirator. 'It's been a pleasure, Cypher,' he said, 'surreal and unexpectedly painful, but a pleasure.'

'No troubles, friend,' was Cypher's simple reply. With that, James strode towards the café's door and left.

He paused for a moment outside, pulling out his phone and quickly tapping out a text to Alice. He'd go over the details with her later on, but for now he thought she should know that things were looking up. At least, as up as they could be looking, given the circumstances.

I've met with the guy and he's been a great help. Will tell you more later, but for now things are looking positive. -James

Sam awoke to find himself lying in the middle of a room. It took him a while to come to his senses again, but after he was able to piece together the events which had lead to this moment, he realised where he was. He was in a prison cell.

It was cold and uninviting, not that cells could ever be said to be warm and welcoming. It was a small concrete cubicle, only a few meters wide and a few meters deep, but the ceilings were fairly high. If this were listed on a London property website, they'd make a big feature out of the high ceilings, regardless of the state of the rest of the place.

In the corner towards the back of the cell was a foam mattress, no more than an inch thick, with a single thin blanket draped over the top of it. Whoever had placed Sam in this cell hadn't had the courtesy to place him on his would-be bed. Not that he minded, though, because the blanket was clearly old and there were several stains on it which Sam didn't dare imagine what they might be. In the opposite corner sat a metal bucket, presumably the makeshift toilet. Mercifully, the bucket was empty.

Struggling to his feet, Sam staggered towards the door. His feet and hands were no longer tied, but he could still feel the soreness from where he'd been bound. Everything hurt, and it was an effort just to stand, but he wasn't just going to lay back and accept his fate. Lifting one bruised hand up, he slammed on the metal door of the cell.

'Hello?! Anyone there?!' He shouted through the door, slamming it with his palm as hard as he could. The metal clanged and echoed in the cell as Sam repeatedly hit the door, but there was no other noise. Eventually, when his hands were starting to feel even more bruised and swollen, Sam relented.

He slumped to the floor, defeated.

Chapter VI

'I'm bloody well coming with you, James!' Alice shouted as James made his way towards his car.

James had met with Alice in Islington that evening to let her know everything he'd learned from Cypher, and to inform her of the current plan of action. He had asked her to stay at home, where it was safe, until the mission was complete. She had refused. At great lengths, James had told her about the underground facility, Cypher's story, and not least the allegedly unkillable inhuman agents who act without remorse, and emphasised exactly why it was imperative she stayed out of harm's way. Again, she refused. He asked her if she heard him say the bit about the unkillable agents, and apparently she had.

She's either incredibly stupid or incredibly brave, James had thought. As Sam Hain's accomplice, it was almost certainly the bravery. He could respect that, and he admired her willingness to take part in something so dangerous and potentially put herself at risk for the good of another. That wasn't going to make him change his mind, though.

Unlocking the doors of his car, James stood by

the driver's side and watched as Alice caught up with him. 'Alice, I've already said to you, it's too dangerous. Please, go home.'

'Why is it too dangerous for me, but not too dangerous for you, hm?' She didn't mean to be so confrontational, especially when the idea of what they were about to do scared her beyond belief. After everything that had happened since Sam had told her that he was being followed, Alice was feeling more than highly strung. She hadn't been able to focus on anything all day, just waiting to hear whether James was on to something, and the stress and worry had consumed her. She wasn't just going to sit idly by when she could be out helping to rescue Sam.

'Listen,' James began, attempting to sound as calming and reassuring as possible, hoping he didn't sound patronising, 'Sam wouldn't want you getting yourself into any unnecessary danger. He couldn't bear losing someone like you. And I wouldn't be able to forgive myself if anything happened to you, too.'

He was right. Sam wouldn't want Alice endangering herself, and she knew it. But she also knew that Sam needed their help, and as far as Alice was concerned there was no debate; she was going to help. In her mind, there was not an alternative.

'James, I've had a shadow being live in my head, I've stared into a Void portal, I have looked into the eyes of a butcher's decapitated head and I have been attacked by re-animated pig carcasses,' she rattled off as she opened the passenger-side door of the car, 'it's not my first adventure. I'm coming.' There was no excitement or intrigue with this adventure though; only a terrifying sinking feeling in the pit of her stomach, and her heart beat heavily in her throat.

The car doors slammed shut as Alice and James seated themselves. With an exaggerated and exasperated sigh, James turned to face Alice and smiled warmly. 'You know, you remind me of my sister,' he said, 'she could be infuriatingly obstinate sometimes, too.'

'Is it really being obstinate when it's the right thing to do?' Alice retorted with a slight smirk.

'Yup, just like Lorna,' James muttered, and he turned the key in the ignition. The car growled to life, and they snaked out into the stream of traffic heading down the road and towards Regent's Park. Towards the Hub.

They pulled up on Prince Albert Road on the north-west side of Regent's Park a little after ten o'clock. The drive had been a relatively short one, and the two of them had spent most of it in silent nerves and quiet contemplation. Neither James or Alice were looking forward to what they were about to do, but they both knew what had to be done. The crumpled up greatcoat in the backseat of the car, with the fedora hat resting on top of it, served as a constant reminder.

Waiting on the corner of Avenue Road, by two pillars which marked one of the gateways to the park, stood a bald man in an old army coat. He waved cheerily at the car as they arrived and parked on the opposite side of the road.

Before getting out of the car, James turned to face Alice. She carried on staring directly ahead, presumably preparing herself as much as she possibly could.

'Ready?' He asked.

'As I'll ever be,' Alice sighed, and they both stepped out of the car, making their way to meet Cypher.

'Alright, mate,' Cypher greeted James, and he tipped an imaginary hat towards Alice, 'enchanté, m'lady. I'll be your tour guide for this evenin'.'

'Alice, this is Cypher,' James said, waving his bandaged hand towards the bald man.

Alice eyed him warily. From what James had told her about their confederate, she wasn't looking forward to placing her trust in an unhinged conspirator. She was nervous enough about the whole situation, without throwing a madman into the mix; she affectionately referred to Sam as mad, but overall he was harmless - if, to put it politely, unique - but she worried that this Cypher was decidedly further along the madness spectrum. Smiling politely, Alice gave the man a cursory 'hello.'

'Now listen, you ain't got nothin' to worry about, darlin',' Cypher said, 'we're going to get your friend out of there all hunky dory.' He leaned forward and touched her arm reassuringly. 'I've got a plan!'

Cypher had explained his plan as they walked

over the bridge crossing the canal, which ran along the perimeter of the park's northern side, and onto the Outer Circle road. From the road, they would climb over the small iron fence into a densely wooded area, using the foliage for cover during their approach. Bearing east beyond the trees, they would stick to the trees and shrubbery around the northern edge of a rugby pitch until they reached a footpath. There would only be a small group of trees between them and the Hub at this point and, Cypher emphasised, moving close to the ground and using what cover they could find would be imperative. From this small cluster of trees, the entrance to the Hub would be visible, and they could assess the next phase of the plan: infiltration.

They had agreed to the plan and, checking over their shoulders to make sure that no-one was watching, one by one they hopped over the iron fence and into the thicket. Beyond the fence, the trees and shrubbery were wild and overgrown, and the trio had to wade through the dense undergrowth as they snuck themselves over the perimeter of Regent's Park. Twigs snapped and dead leaves crunched underfoot with each careful, trudging step. Alice clutched Sam's hat close to her, and for reasons she couldn't quite explain she found holding onto it was somehow reassuring.

It wasn't long before they had cleared the thicket and found themselves on the edge of a clearing which appeared to stretch away into blackness. The dark shapes of trees marked the horizon, silhouetted against the clear night sky, dotted with the faint light of countless stars. In the distance, the warm golden lights of London glowed almost in defiance of the cold bluish-black of night.

Under the cold white glow of the moon, they could just about make out the well-kept grounds of what must be the rugby pitch. Directly ahead of them and no more than a hundred yards away was another smaller cluster of trees and the very faint hint of a concrete footpath. Cypher signalled for them to move around the outside of the rugby pitch, sticking close to the treeline, and to keep low. Crouching, they slowly and carefully arced around the pitch and towards the path, looping around behind trees where possible, until they eventually made it to the pathway.

The terrain was irritatingly flat, and the only cover they had on their final approach was from the small, sparse cluster of trees which separated the footpath from the Hub. Had it not been nearing midnight and they were under the cover of the darkness, the three of them would have been clearly visible. Cypher gestured at the trees and flattened himself against one of the trunks. Alice and James followed suit. One by one, they peeled away from the trees and scurried towards the next one, advancing forward until it was eventually insight.

On top of a small, artificial-looking mound sat the Hub. It was a squat, circular structure, made mostly of glass and metal, and it put Alice in mind of a spaceship from an old science fiction film, almost like a classic flying saucer. Despite its sci-fi appearance, the UFO-like glass building was in fact a café during the day. Beneath it, a large opening was cut into the side of the mound, leading to a small concrete tunnel into the space beneath the Hub. Standing just within the entrance of this concrete passageway, Alice saw two men. Both were tall and slender, wearing finely tailored black suits, and narrow sunglasses covered their eyes despite the fact it was night. Their appearance was all the more unsettling tonight, standing stock still and staring straight ahead like statue-esque sentinels.

Alice mimed to James and Cypher, gesturing around the tree to where the guards were stood and holding up two fingers. Creeping around the trees to a position just outside of the Men in Black's vision, the three of them huddled together.

'There's two of them, three of us,' Cypher whispered chirpily.

'You're not suggesting a full-frontal assault, are you?'

'Why not? It'll be easy peasy lemon-squeezy. Listen, we get closer to the buggers, then we rush 'em! Bish-bash-bosh, and they're out like a light. Luvvly jubbly!'

'Does he always talk like this?' Alice turned to James, raising a concerned eyebrow.

'I'm afraid so, yes,' James said frankly. 'It's not too late, Alice. You don't need to follow us in.'

'Actually, I think it might be too late now,' Alice said. Her eyes didn't meet James's, instead she was staring beyond him and towards the Hub with a shocked expression. When he turned, James noticed Cypher was no longer by the side of them, and with a sinking feeling in the pit of his stomach he heard a distant shout.

'Alright, chaps! Which way to the top secret base?'

Cypher had sprinted right up to the two Men in Black, and seemed to be tauntingly dancing in front of them before breaking into a run further away into the park. One of the agents gave chase, sprinting after him at full pelt.

'Shit!' James spat, and without another word he too broke into a run, arcing around outside of the agent's vision, quickly making his way from the trees to the side of the Hub. It was a narrow window of opportunity, but James knew he had to act fast to make the most of the situation. With only one agent between them and the Hub, the odds were a little more in their favour. And Cypher had forced his hand by jumping straight in, so it was now or never.

Skirting around the edge of the mound, James started to approach the remaining agent from behind. He moved fast but quietly, and when he was an arm's reach away he tapped the agent on the shoulder. The Man in Black turned around stoically, only to be met with a right hook to the face. He immediately crumpled and fell to the floor, unconscious. Kneeling down, James fished around inside the agent's jacket for anything which might be useful, and retrieved a keycard from the breast pocket. With a beckoning wave, James gestured for Alice to come over.

'That was all very sudden,' Alice said as she jogged over to the entrance of the Hub, 'what's the plan now? What about Cypher?'

'I can only assume he knows what he's doing,' James muttered, and he hesitated for a moment. He'd noticed the grip of a handgun sticking out of a holster around the agent's waist, and after a moment's consideration James took the weapon. It was shiny and sleek, but he didn't bother inspecting it further and simply secured it beneath his belt. Better to go in there armed than to come back out unarmed and be met by a man with a gun and a black eye. Standing up, James brandished the keycard he'd found to Alice. 'Now,' he said, 'we let ourselves in.'

Inside, the area beneath the Hub wasn't much to look at. Concrete corridors lined with storage lockers led blandly to the central circular area directly beneath the café. In the very centre, a spiral staircase wound upwards to the café above, and around the room several doors ran off into other rooms. The Hub was certainly larger than it would have suggested from the outside. Peering cautiously into the other rooms, James and Alice discovered two very empty function rooms, but nothing of any interest.

There was, however, one door which separated itself from the rest. At a glance, it wasn't any different from the others, a simple grey door with two circular windows, but instead of having a number on the wall by the side of it, there was the familiar hieroglyph of the Was Sceptre. Beneath the symbol was a simple card reader.

'Not very secretive, is it?' Alice mused as they approached the door.

'I suppose they don't have to be. If you've come this far, you either know what's behind this door, or you don't even give it a second thought.' James tapped the keycard against the reader by the side of the door. It beeped merrily, followed by the *click* of a door unlocking.

They stepped through the door into another concrete corridor. This one was even more desolate than the last; completely empty, save for the elevator waiting for them at the end of the corridor. Alice and James set foot in the elevator and, almost as if operating on autopilot, she pressed a button. Other than the standard range of buttons (doors close/open, emergency, and the mysterious unmarked fourth button which could do anything from call maintenance to transport you all the way down to the seventh circle of Hell) there were only two operational buttons: Up and Down. It was the latter which Alice pressed. The elevator doors closed, and with a jolt they were heading down.

The journey down felt like an eternity, probably not least because of Alice and James's rising anxiety, but also because they were heading quite some way underground. It wasn't like taking the lift down to the food court in Oxford Street's Marks and Spencer as much as it was like trying to get to the twentieth floor of a high-rise building; if that building were structurally inverted and almost exclusively underground.

Alice had imagined her apprehension would

slowly dissolve as she got more involved with the infiltration, as she often overcame her fear when on a case with Sam, but this time was different. A solid lump stuck in her throat and her stomach felt heavy and uneasy. She was starting to feel numb and lightheaded, and she nervously toyed with Sam's hat in her hands. Despite his peculiarities and haphazard approach, the occult detective always seemed to have things under control in the end. This was a situation far from Sam's, or indeed anyone else's, control and Alice felt like they were in over their heads.

Stood by the side of her, James idly nursed his bandaged hand. He was lost in his own thoughts. The minute the doors opened, they would find themselves in the heart of a Regents' facility from where - if Cypher's story was anything to go by - very few people returned to see the light of day. The thought of that was driving James forward, to defy the odds and get his friend out, but it didn't make it any easier. The sensation of the gun tucked into his waistband was not providing him with any reassurance.

The elevator came to a stop, and the doors slid open.

Peering out from just within the doors, James and Alice were unsurprised to be greeted by the sight of yet another corridor. What did surprise them was that it looked decidedly older than the floor above. The off-white plaster walls were cracked and stained in places, and where it had started to peel and crumble away it revealed it was covering brickwork which looked even older. It vaguely resembled an old World War II bunker or a disused Underground station. Fluorescent strip lights lined the arched ceiling, casting an incongruously bright light on the dingy hallway. The place gave Alice a sense of deja vu as images from her dream echoed in the back of her mind. It was more than eerily similar.

It seemed to be just as deserted as the level above, with no sign of the Men in Black - or indeed anyone else - in sight, which came as a welcome relief. On either side of the corridor there was a small alcove, each with a doorway, and further along two more hallways ran off to the left and right. At the far end there was a set of double doors, and James suspected that this was where they needed to be heading.

They held position for a moment, staring out and into the corridor, watching for any signs of activity. When James felt confident that they weren't about to be ambushed, he tapped Alice on the arm and lead the way out of the elevator. They hurried forwards in silence, eyes and ears open for any hint of danger, and even their lightest of footsteps put them on edge, fearing they'd be discovered at any moment. Alice was starting to feel as if she was in a nightmare she couldn't wake up from, sneaking through this place so far underground and with its eerily decrepit hallways. It was a far cry from the glass, metal and concrete of the modern building above. The fear of being discovered was all the more palpable now, and she was certain that even the slightest mistake would not only cost them the opportunity to find Sam, but ensure that they would never see the light of day again. The thought did not instill her with confidence.

The doors at the end of the corridor began to open, and without a moment's hesitation James ducked into one of the alcoves, dragging Alice with him. She almost yelped in surprise as she felt herself being pulled off-balance, but caught herself before she could make a noise. James pushed her tightly against the inside of the wall, and he flattened himself against it too, holding a finger to his lips.

Footsteps. At first it sounded like one person walking, but as James listened closely to the echoing footfall he could hear it was two people walking in almost perfect unison. The footsteps were coming closer. And closer. James's breath felt tight in his chest. He didn't risk glancing around the corner to see how close they were, but they sounded much too close for his comfort. Glancing at the door to the side of them, James carefully pulled it open just enough to slide in and ushered Alice inside. He closed it just as carefully, slowly easing the handle upwards, and he was relieved when the latch didn't click as it slid into place.

The room they now found themselves in was large, dimly lit by a couple of flickering light-bulbs, and packed full with boxes and crates. Narrow pathways wound through the piles of boxes like a maze, and James and Alice snaked their way through, deeper into the storage room. Peering out from among the boxes and the shadowy recesses were ancient statues of unearthly looking beings, made all the more sinister in the low light of the room. Some bore screaming demonic faces, others more composed and regal but far from human in appearance, and some resembling rejected concepts for Egyptian gods. Alice tried not to look at them. It wasn't just that they looked as if they'd be at home in the British Museum's Exhibit of Creepiest Deities, but she had the very distinct impression that they were staring at her.

'Come on,' James whispered, 'I think I can see a door behind the hippalectryon.' It was a sentence he had never even considered he might say, but he wasn't wrong. Around the corner, on which stood the statue of a creature which bore the front half of a horse and the hind of a rooster, there was another door. They made their way towards the door - Alice eyeing the rooster-horse suspiciously as they crept past it - and, cautiously, James pushed it open and slid out into the corridor.

They were now just around the corner from the double doors. It was still and quiet in the corridor again, the sound of footsteps no longer echoing off of the walls, and after a moment of listening out for any noise James began to lead the way. He stuck close to the wall, almost skimming along it until he reached the corner. Pinning himself against the wall, James could almost see back down the corridor they'd entered from. The lift's doors were closed, and he assumed that whoever had been coming down that corridor had taken it back up to the surface. He tilted his head to the side and cautiously tried to look around the corner.

The double doors were open, leading into a large ovular chamber. It was brightly lit and looked like it had fared better over the years than the rest of the facility; the white walls seemed almost new, and the floor appeared to be a large metal walkway. It opened up in the very middle of the room, presumably overlooking the chamber's lower level. Computer banks, terminals and desks ran around the edge of the central opening, and on the far wall there was a large display which appeared to show a map of London. Numerous lights and blips flashed across the map. Silhouetted against the display stood two figures with the poise and stillness of suit department mannequins. They didn't appear to be facing towards the corridor, their attentions focussed on the display, and James saw the opportunity. He scurried around the corner and into the chamber, crouching behind the first group of desks.

Without thinking, Alice followed suit and almost froze when she noticed the two figures on the opposite side of the room. She quickly ducked down and joined James behind the desk, where he greeted her with a finger held against his pursed lips. Slowly, he glanced over the top of the desk. They were still there, facing the display and with their backs turned to them, seemingly unaware of the two intruders.

James quickly skirted around the end of the desk, keeping low while he advanced along the row of terminals before taking cover behind the next work station. He was now halfway across the chamber, and he couldn't have been more than ten yards away from the two agents. They remained stock still, monitoring their display. If he stood any chance of finding where Sam was being held, he'd need to access one of the computers, and he knew he couldn't risk that when the Men in Black were present. He glanced back around towards Alice, and signalled for her to stay where she was. She nodded with fearful agreement. She felt glued to the spot anyway, and hiding beneath a desk seemed like the safest place to be.

James took another quick glance over towards the agents, and felt his hand graze the grip of the gun. Carefully, he withdrew it from his belt. If push came to shove, he'd be ready.

For the first time since picking it up, James inspected the weapon. It was quite unlike any handgun he'd seen before. The body of the gun was sleek and curved, and made of brushed steel or chrome, giving it an almost science fiction inspired finish. Above the grip was a switch and two light emitting diodes, and there was no sign of a traditional firearm's hammer. Where one would normally expect the gun's barrel to be was instead a long transparent cylinder, revealing the unusual firing mechanism inside. Five copper rods ran along the length of the inside of the cylinder, culminating at the muzzle. A large quartzite stone was held in place between these rods, which stretched the length of the cylindrical chamber, from the crystal's base - secured within the body of the gun, just above the trigger - to the point, which incorporated itself into the muzzle. James eyed the gun curiously. It almost looked like a weaponised version of Sam's energy probe wand. He flicked what he presumed was the safety switch.

The gun made a short, high-pitched whining noise before settling into a consistent gentle hum. One of the little diodes shone green.

This was shortly followed by a very similar noise, and the measured voice of a man saying 'don't move.'

James looked up to the see the tall figure of one of the agents standing over him, and the same other-worldly gun pointing at his head. He knew the agent would pull the trigger before he even had a chance to raise his weapon in response, and as much as he was intrigued by how this device worked, he thought it best if he wasn't on the receiving end.

'Looks like we have an intruder,' the agent said flatly. 'How did you get in?'

'How'd ya think he got in? In-tru-da window?' An unexpectedly chipper cockney voice called out from the direction of the corridor. There was the loud crackling buzz of electricity, and suddenly a bolt of white-purple energy shot across James's vision, striking the agent squarely in the chest. He promptly vanished in a plume of smoke, which seemed to surprise the agent in his final fleeting moments of corporeality almost as much as it had surprised James to witness it.

The beam continued to crackle and buzz as the

stream of energy arced above James's head. Sparks flew and the nearby computer terminals popped and sizzled, and James took shelter beneath one of the desks. He looked around urgently, trying to see if he could spot Alice. Through another hail of sparks he could see her, also huddled beneath a desk and hugging her knees. There was a shout from the remaining agent, and a reciprocating beam of energy briefly fired back before both streams of lightning ceased. The lights of the chamber flickered uncertainly in the ensuing calm. Everything fell silent.

'Looks like I got 'ere just in time, hey?' The voice broke the silence, and the grinning face of Cypher appeared as he knelt down by the desk. He was met with the terrified, wide-eyed face of Alice. Her lips trembled involuntarily as she managed a small and nervous nod. 'It's alright, love, I vapourised 'em both!' Cypher said, waving the strange gun cheerily, and although he meant it in a reassuring way, it was anything but.

Alice was uneasy on her feet as she unfurled from beneath the desk. Cypher had held out his hand to help her up, but it wasn't until she was standing that she realised how much she had actually needed the support. Her whole body was shaking as fear and adrenaline coursed through every fibre of her being, her knees were weak, and she felt as if her legs had turned to jelly. Lurching forwards, Alice steadied herself and clutched one of the desks for balance, squeezing her eyes tightly shut. The mayhem had finished almost as quickly as it had started, but it was going to take longer than that for her nerves to calm down. She struggled to catch her breath as another wave of panic washed over her, and she tried to focus on taking regular, deep breaths, and not how close to death she had just been.

A couple of yards away, James was staggering to his feet too. He seemed more dazed and confused than anything else, and he welcomed the sight of Cypher with a lackluster wave. He quickly looked around the room, swaying as he turned his head one way and the other. There was no trace of the Men in Black whatsoever. No bodies, no suddenly empty suits, not even a pile of ash. Nothing. It was as if they simply ceased to be.

'Ah, see you nabbed yourself one of these beauts too, hey Jimmy-boy,' Cypher said, casually waving his gun about as if it were a flag. James flinched every time the muzzle was vaguely pointed in his direction. 'Got mine from the bastard who chased me. Lovely bit of kit.'

'You... You vapourised them?' Alice uttered.

'It's alright, they ain't real. Not like you or I. They're thoughtforms them Regents willed into bein' to do their dirty work. They ain't people, strictly speaking; they exist only to serve their purpose, like worker bees and investment bankers. Give 'em a zap and *poof*, the idea is gone.'

'You can't kill an idea, though,' James said.

'Ah, you're a canny one,' Cypher replied, waving finger-guns in James's direction, 'you're quite right. Can't kill an idea; ideas exist in a realm beyond the physical. But you can disrupt 'em. You can knock one of them Men in Black bastards out with enough force, and with a blast from one o' these tezzers of theirs you can vapourise their manifestation. The core idea of the Men in Black ain't gone, mind you, they'll rematerialise eventually, but you can hinder 'em and blast 'em out of this plane of existence for a little while.'

James nodded dumbly. He hadn't quite believed Cypher at the café when he'd said that they weren't real, at least not to the full extent. It sounded too absurd to believe that the Men in Black were ideas given form, but seeing the agent evaporate in front of his eyes was as close as he was likely to get to solid evidence. Although 'solid' probably wasn't the most accurate adjective, given the context. Even so, it was no less unsettling to witness the agent vapourising with that knowledge, and going by the pale look on Alice's face that explanation didn't do much in the way of putting her at ease either.

'So, if we got caught in the…?' Alice waved her hands around as she tried to find the words. Her mind was more than muddled from the panic, and she was struggling to get her thoughts straight. Even though they were now safe from the brief crossfire, having to cower beneath a desk while men fired lightning bolts from pistols at each other was not an experience that was going to be leaving her any time soon. 'Would we be, y'know, gone?'

Cypher shook his head emphatically. 'Oh no, not gone. You'd be unconscious for a bit and have a wicked bad headache and muscle-ache when you came to, maybe some nasty burns where you was hit, but not gone. It's a stun gun more than anythin', but got just enough ampage to disrupt thoughtforms. Although,' he added, and tweaked one of the switches on the gun, 'up the output and ya can kill an elephant stone dead.'

While Cypher was busy explaining the functionality of the gun to a very on-edge Alice, James took the opportunity to access one of the computer terminals. He tapped rapidly at the keyboard as he sifted through the directory, searching for anything relevant. Several folders and documents were password encoded, but he did get access to a file which seemed to display a map of the facility. The first thing which struck James was how similar in shape the floorplan was to the Ankh, an ancient Egyptian symbol of life. Considering the Regents identified themselves with another ancient Egyptian symbol, he didn't think it was all that surprising. The second thing which struck him was that, marked on the lower level immediately beneath them, was a label which simply read: 'containment.'

James looked up from the computer screen and turned to face the other two. Cypher was waving the 'tezzer' gun around while explaining in great detail the welt he had on his back after he was zapped by the Men in Black one time. Standing opposite him, a very pale Alice stood with her arms crossed and had the expression of someone who's just realised they're about to be hit in the face by a cricket ball. 'Are we right above the cells?' James asked, interrupting Cypher's story much to Alice's relief.

'Yessir, we gotta head down there.' Cypher pointed to the large opening in the middle of the floor of the chamber. Railings ran around the perimeter of the opening, and at the far end of the room a flight of steps led down to the level below. From where they were, the three were able to peer over the railings to the lower level. There were fewer terminals and desks below, only a couple of pieces of machinery and relays which connected to the terminals on the upper level. A tangle of cables wound their way around the room and towards the centre where, at the very heart of the chamber, stood an unearthly shape.

A small dias was raised up from the floor, and from it four narrow, curving prongs stuck out, arching upwards and inwards. The very points of the prongs culminated in the middle some ten feet above the ground, making the structure's overall shape almost resemble the outline of an egg. At a glance it seemed to be carved from a black stone, but where the smooth surface reflected the light of the room it appeared to shimmer and gleam with hints of deep purples and turquoise greens. It was like looking at the surface of the water in a clear and deep ocean. There was something ethereally beautiful about, yet also something forbidding and disquieting. At the base of the prongs the extraordinary met the ordinary, and great metal clamps were secured around the otherworldly monument, with wire and cables snaking around it.

It was an unusual thing to behold, its unearthly

form jutting out from amongst desks, computers and cables, almost like something poking its way through from another universe.

'This is what they're here for,' Cypher announced as if he were a tour guide, 'this gert thing. Sounds like an amazin' idea on paper; shame it snaps fragile human minds in 'alf like twigs.'

'Something about it seems familiar, somehow,' Alice said as they drew closer to it. She could make out the shapes of strange symbols carved into its base and along the prongs, a string of angular sigils which looked like nothing on Earth. In the centre of the monument's base a spiral-like pattern wound around itself. 'What is it?'

'No-one really knows,' he replied, 'but they're doin' their damnedest to learn its true purpose. So far, it works by rippin' an 'ole in the fabric of reality as a kind of interstitial cross-dimensional gateway.' He walked up to the monument and slammed his hand against one of the prongs. The structure stood firm, barely even acknowledging the force of Cypher's hit, but beneath the black stone surface a cloud of purples and greens rippled like droplets in a pool of water.

Ripping a hole in the fabric of reality… Alice mused as she stared transfixed by the rippling colours. There was something unsettling about the otherworldly structure, but also something terrifyingly alluring. It was then, as she looked into the depths of the rippling beneath the solid stone, that she realised why it seemed familiar. She glimpsed the gaping nothingness that she and Sam had found once before, the wound in reality which had been torn open by a Void crystal. The engravings on the monument here were more than reminiscent of the symbols carved into the crystal. 'This is a Void portal,' Alice said aloud as the revelation dawned on her.

'The lady knows 'er stuff, hey,' Cypher replied with a wink, 'you're spot on, love. This is Project Voidwalker. Bane of my fugged up life.'

'They use this thing to open a gateway, and then… They send you through it? How does it work?' James asked, intrigued.

'Nah, they don't open no gate, nothin' so neat 'n' tidy. They zap it full of power and punch a bloody great hole through dimensions, like jabbin' scissors through cardboard.' Cypher looked at the gateway of Project Voidwalker with disdain. Its smooth black surface seemed to stare back at him coldly. He shook his head as if an insect were bothering him, and he turned to start making his way towards a door at the far end of the chamber. 'Detainment cells are right through 'ere.'

Cypher led them away from the gateway and into the cells. The corridor was dark and dank, its plain concrete walls occasionally broken up by the doors to cells. Most of them were open, and as the trio walked past each room they looked in out of curiosity. Each cell was incredibly small, and aside from the thin mattresses laid out on the floors, the cells were entirely empty. Anyone detained in them would have nothing but the four concrete walls. That would have been their world.

'Bloody hate this place,' Cypher spat. He skulked ahead of James and Alice, leering into each room they passed. One door refused to open as Cypher tried it, and after a few inquiring pushes he decided to slide the viewing grate open and peek in. No sooner had he put his face to the now-open grate, Cypher jumped back and slid the cover shut again. A moment later, there was a very loud metallic thud from the other side of the door. 'Don't think ya friend's in that one,' he announced, wide-eyed.

Tentatively, James and Alice approached the door and slid the viewing grate open again. The grate didn't allow them much of a look into the room, and in the dim light they could barely see anything. Then, at the back of the cell, Alice spotted the shape of a person. The person was huddled up in the corner, but when they sensed they were being watched they looked up. It was at that moment that Alice instinctively clutched hold of James's sleeve and let out a slight whimpering noise as she tried to suppress a scream.

The person looking back at them wasn't quite a person. Outwardly, it appeared as human as anyone else, but it stared back at them from the dark with vibrant yellow eyes. The pupils were thin black slits, and when the thing blinked, it blinked sideways. The almost human-looking face started to contort into an unnatural smile, until the creature's grin literally stretched from ear to ear, revealing rows of razor-sharp teeth. It snapped and hissed at them, and James quickly pulled the grate shut again.

The door banged several more times as the thing threw itself at the inside of its prison.

'What the hell was that?' Alice asked, her voice wavering. She was suddenly feeling quite sick and light-headed again.

'Voidwalker,' Cypher said dispassionately. 'Sendin' folk through that portal, there's no tellin' what's gonna happen. Some go mad, have their minds snapped in two, but sometimes people come back... Changed. That,' he said, pointing towards the metal door, which now emitted a low snarling sound, 'that ain't human. It may look it, but somethin' else has piggybacked its way 'ere.'

The other occupied cells hardly seemed any better off. Of all the doors in the corridor, which looped around the operations chamber, only five of them had anything in the cells behind them. As they checked each door, sliding the grates open to look inside, they were greeted by a series of snarls, hisses and woops. Alice had to keep reminding herself that the nightmare would be over as soon as they found Sam. Seeing, even hearing, these things which weren't quite human was making her skin crawl, and she was relatively sure her heart was now going into overdrive. Upon the fifth door they looked into, they were greeted with a surprisingly courteous 'oh, hello!'

'Sam!' Alice exclaimed, and a sudden rush of relief washed over her. Cypher began to fiddle with the locks and bolts, the clanking metal echoing throughout the corridor as he unlocked the door. Eventually, with the final bolt removed, the door swung open.

'Alice! Thank God you're here. I've been clicking my heels together, saying 'there's no place like home' for ages!'

Alice could tell he was just putting on a jovial front, and in his eyes she could see the glistening of tears welling up. He lunged forward, flinging his arms wide and taking her in a tight embrace. It was a hug of sudden, inexorable relief. She couldn't begin to imagine the desperation he must have felt being trapped in that cell, but the rush of relief wasn't lost on her and she returned the hug with an equally tight grip.

'And you brought my hat too!' He exclaimed when he eventually released her from his arms. Alice had almost forgotten she had been carrying Sam's hat with her; she'd been holding onto it for so long now it hadn't really occurred to her. She handed it over to him, and he perched it on his head. He finally was starting to feel more like himself. All that was missing was the coat, and he'd feel whole again.

Stepping forward, Sam took James's hand in a firm shake, before pulling him in for a hug too. 'Honestly, you have no bloody idea how happy I am to see you both. It is terrifyingly boring in that cell. There's nothing to do. Not even one of the Men in Black spooks for company.' He turned and saw Cypher standing by the door. 'And you…' Sam scrunched his face and sucked the air through his teeth as he racked his brains trying to recognise the bald man in the military jacket. The silence in the middle of his sentence was beginning to stretch on for too long, and Sam concluded it was more than likely that he didn't know who this man was. 'And you... Person. Thank you for whatever it is you did.'

'This is Cypher. He provided the intel, helped us get inside, even saved our skin not that long ago,' James said in way of introducing their accomplice. Cypher took an elaborate and exaggerated bow.

'At ya service, sir!' He extended his hand and shook Sam's enthusiastically. 'I spent more time in this place than I'd care to tell ya, so helpin' another soul outta here seemed like the least I could do.'

'Then I'm incredibly grateful for your help too, Cypher,' Sam said, and he tipped his hat to him. He turned to face all three of them, and he was almost overwhelmed by the feelings of relief and joy such a simple sight could bring. 'I feared they might have got to you as well. Inside those four walls, after a while it's impossible to imagine you'll ever see the light of day again, let alone the people close to you. I-'

'There they are! Get them!' A shout from down the corridor cut Sam's sentence short. Two Men in Black had appeared through one of the doorways and reached for their weapons. They fired.

'I'll finish my sentence later,' Sam said as a bolt of purplish energy zipped past them, scorching the wall behind his head. 'Run!'

They ran. Cypher and James drew their guns too, and fired over their shoulders at their pursuers. The beams hit far from their mark and sparked harmlessly off of the concrete walls. At the very least it slowed down the agents' pursuit. The Men in Black fired back, taking potshots at the escapees as they fled. Beams crossed, and the colliding energy flared in sizzling balls of light at the heart of the crossfire.

'Why do you have ray guns?!' Sam shouted. Energy bolts flew chaotically around them. Beams buzzed and crackled with electric ferocity. Sparks erupted from the walls.

Agent Smith took extra care in lining up his next shot. With any luck, he thought, he'd stun Sam Hain and put a burning hole through that stupid hat of his. *Might even kill him.* He aimed, and pulled the trigger. White-purple energy arced from the gun's muzzle, cutting its way through the air with a crackling buzz. With moments to spare, the four escaped through the door into the main chamber, slamming it shut behind them. A shower of sparks burst as the beam hit the metal door, leaving a burn mark at exactly head-height. Smith cursed under his breath and continued the chase.

On the other side of the door, Cypher tipped over a server bank as a temporary barricade, heaving it against the chambers double doors. It wouldn't hold the agents back for long, but they needed all the time they could get. Sam had momentarily slowed to take a look at the Voidwalker gateway in the middle of the chamber. He gawped perplexedly at the unearthly structure. 'Is that an interstitial cross-dimensional Void gateway?'

'Funny time to ask questions,' Cypher retorted,

and he fired a stream of vibrant energy into the core of the gateway. Electricity began to surge up the prongs, winding around them like ethereal serpents. It started to hum ominously. Connected cables and machinery sparked violently, and a couple of the computers on the lower level blew out, smoke rising from the terminals.

The four of them reached the top of the stairs and looked back towards the way they had just come. The doors shook and rattled as the agents tried to force their way through, but the server bank was proving to be quite stubborn. It had moved less than an inch, although it was slowly scraping bit by bit across the floor with each subsequent ramming of the doors. The computers and machinery below were the very image of devastation, and at the heart of it all the gateway seemed to be glowing.

Wasting no time, Cypher ran over to one of the computers on the upper level and began typing frantically. A window which appeared to display technical readouts popped up on the screen, and several of its meters had escalated from green, straight through amber, and threatening to break into the red at an alarming rate.

'What're ya waitin' for, for Chrissakes?! Get movin'!' He shouted, as Alice, Sam and James hovered, hesitating by the way out, waiting for him to follow.

'What are you doing?' Sam demanded. 'In a couple of minutes they're going to get through that bloody door. We need to leave, now.'

'In two minutes, that ain't gonna matter, friend. I got some unfinished business with these chaps.'

'What's going to happen in two minutes?' James asked, and he ran back towards Cypher.

Alice looked nervously down at the doors as the agents on the other side were continuing to ram their way through. A gap was starting to appear in the doorway. They'd be through in no time. She clutched on to Sam's arm.

'You won't be 'ere to find out, that's what!' Cypher exclaimed, and he tried to shoo James away. 'By the by, mister Hain, I wiped that there arrest warrant thing off their server. The Fuzz shouldn't be troublin' you,' he nodded his head back towards the ever-opening door, 'can't say as much 'bout them bastards.'

'Thank you, Cypher,' Sam said. 'Really, thank you.'

'Been a pleasure, sir, now get the buggery outta here. You ain't got long.'

Alice nodded and gave her thanks as well, and she started to lead Sam away by the arm, pulling him along and towards the lift back to the surface. They hadn't made it this far, having gone through everything they'd had to endure, only for it all to go wrong again. She was going to make sure of that.

'Sorry 'bout ya hand, again,' Cypher said, turning to James, 'jus' don't want ya thinkin' I's the kinda man who goes about stabbin' people in the 'and all the time.' He flashed him a quick smile.

'Cypher, what happens in two minutes?' James

insisted. Ribbons of energy coursed along the structure of the Voidwalker gateway, and unless he was mistaken, James was sure it was building up to something.

'I turned off their poncey safety measures, rigged that thing to overload. The fugger's gonna blow any minute now, takin' this God-forsaken shit 'ole with it.'

The door eventually burst open, and immediately agents Smith and Jones began firing up at James and Cypher. They both ducked down, narrowly avoiding the energy beam as it streamed over them, and Cypher fired a quick warning shot in the general direction of their adversaries. More crackling of electricity filled the air, and an alarm started to sound as the gateway's readings fluctuated wildly in the red. There was a loud booming sound, and a quick look down to the level below revealed that the gateway was active. A swirling vortex had formed between the prongs, and bolts of lightning lashed out from its centre and around the room.

'You're bloody mad-'

'I know that,' Cypher interrupted.

'We're not leaving you here.'

'Don't you be worryin' 'bout me, Jimmy-boy. This ain't me first cross-dimensional rip, after all. I'll keep 'em busy while you 'n' your friends get out, alright? Never know, me and them monstrosities in those cells might find some peace when this place goes kablooey.' Cypher glanced around the corner and saw the agents trying to make their way up the stairs, and fired another warning shot in their direction. 'Looks like I can finally get me revenge on the bastards. Now go on, off ya pop, you ain't got long now with all this chin-waggin'.'

James hovered in a stunned silence, while the crackling and booming cacophony of the Void gateway's overload started to take its toll on the chamber. The walls were cracking and the ceiling was threatening to collapse, all the while the swirling maw of the Void grew larger, unleashing a raging storm from its heart. Another bolt of energy from the Men in Black's guns surged past James's head, and Cypher pushed him towards the exit.

'Thank you for everything you've done,' James said with a pained smile, 'you mad bastard.'

'I'll see you on the other side, my friend,' Cypher said.

That was the last James saw of him. He sprinted for the elevator at the end of the corridor, and without explaining to either Sam or Alice he shoved them into the lift and slammed the button. Before the doors could close, they heard one last shout coming from the chamber: 'Come on, ya wankers! Bet Voidwalkin' don't seem like such a bright idea now, does it?'

The elevator doors closed, and they felt it start moving up back towards the surface. A few moments later, a muffled but deafeningly loud boom ripped through the air, shaking the lift and almost knocking its occupants off their feet. James sunk despondently into the corner and stared at the floor.

Kneeling by the side of him, Alice gently held his hand, and for the first time that evening she allowed herself the emotional breakdown she'd been holding back. Tears started to roll down her face as the fear, the relief, and the panic overwhelmed her all at once. Sam instinctively crouched beside her, putting his arm around her and cradling her head to his chest. The ride back to ground level was the longest any of them had experienced.

The cold night air was crisp and fresh on their faces when they eventually emerged from the Hub. On the surface, Regent's Park looked entirely unchanged. There was no sign that the explosion below had had any effect on the outside world. Up here, everything seemed so still and quiet. Sam stared up at the twinkling stars and took a deep lungful of the fresh air. It felt good to be back in the real world again. He almost said as such, but thought better of it given the circumstances.

'He was a good man,' James said, 'completely unhinged, but a good man.'

'Mad as a box of frogs,' Sam agreed solemnly. 'Cypher sacrificed everything so we could get out alive, and he managed to take that place down with him. The mark of a true, good - if a tad crazy - man. He gave his life to save mine. You all risked everything to break me out. I won't forget that.

And I'm sure the Regents won't forget what happened here in a hurry, either.'

'He didn't need to die. There was still time. I should've… I should've dragged the obstinate git out with me!' James kicked a wall out of frustration, but it didn't give him the release he was hoping it would. 'I barely even knew him, but it was my fault. I brought him into this, and it got him killed. Too many people suffer because of cock ups like that. It's not right, damn it!' He kicked the wall again, still with no effect other than hurting his foot.

'We couldn't have done it without him,' Alice said sombrely, and she placed her hand on James's arm, 'he helped us more than we could've expected. He didn't need to; he wanted to. You can't beat yourself up over that, there was nothing more you could've done.'

Silence hung heavily in the air. James stared vacantly at the grass. His skin was pale and his eyes black, a curious mix of remorse and anger written across his face. 'I still could've pulled him out with me.'

'I mean no disrespect to the guy, but he wasn't all there, was he?' Alice remarked. 'It was what he wanted. Maybe… Maybe he found his peace. And he helped rescue Sam, and destroyed that horrible place at the same time. That's pretty good if you ask me.'

James nodded sagely. Alice was right; Cypher had given his all and did what he felt to be right. 'Yeah, I suppose,' he said, 'I can't help but feel like

I dragged him into this, but he was more than ready to lend a hand. And after everything those bastards did to him... He got his revenge though, taking them down with him. Hopefully he found some solace in his final act.'

'Still, it doesn't feel like this is over,' Sam mused, staring at the star-studded sky. 'Smith said something about them being more in control of things... This isn't the last we've heard of the Regents, I'm sure of it.' An involuntary shiver shook Sam's body, and it occurred to him that he was still missing his coat. 'Anyway, let's get going, shall we? It's bloody freezing out here.'

The walk back to the car was a quiet and sombre one. The three of them walked in silence, their minds caught somewhere in between the nightmare they'd just been through and the relief that the ordeal was finally over with. At least getting back to the car was easier now they weren't having to sneak through the undergrowth surrounding Regent's Park, and they could walk along the paths and pavements with ease.

When they had got back to the car, Sam had taken his coat from the back seat and draped it over Alice like a blanket for the drive back to Islington. She had started shivering uncontrollably - whether it was the cold or her body was in shock, he couldn't tell - and he figured he could cope without it for a while longer. The weight of the coat had surprised Alice, it was a lot bigger and more unwieldy than it looked, but it was warm and comforting. She sat curled up in the back seat of the car, and watched the glow of the streets rush on by.

These roads, so frequently bustling with traffic, were strangely empty and serene at this time of night. In some ways it was good to get back to the normal world, but she knew it would take a while for her to shake the disquiet and uneasiness from that night. For the time being, though, it was over. Sam Hain was safe, and in spite of everything she and James were okay too. She was thankful for that.

With a slight jolt and the clunking of gears, they pulled up outside of Alice's home. James twisted in the driver's seat, craning his neck around the headrest. 'Thank you for everything, Alice,' he said, straining to face her properly, 'and I'm sorry for everything I've put you through. We soldiered on through, though, hey. You're a star.' He smiled a half-hearted smile, and although he meant it, it was difficult to hide the shadow of remorse. 'You've found a good one, Sam,' he added, turning to his friend who was busy watching a spider which had made its home in the wing-mirror, 'hopefully she'll help keep you out of trouble.'

Alice smiled sweetly back at him, uttering a thank-you and wished him a goodnight, and she unfurled herself from the coat. Shakily, she stepped out of the car and began to make her way around to the front door. She was searching for her keys in the dim light of the street, cursing that nothing could ever be easy when all she wanted to do was get inside and crawl into the safety of her bed, when she heard the sound of feet bounding up behind her.

Turning, she saw Sam Hain standing in the orange glow of the streetlight, looking much more like his usual self. His hat perched on top of his long, curling hair, slanting slightly over his face, and his greatcoat billowed around his ankles in the light breeze.

'There aren't any words for me to tell you how grateful I am,' Sam said, 'so a simple 'thank-you' will have to do.' Expressing genuine gratitude was evidently not something which came easily to Sam Hain, but there was a sincerity behind his eyes and a kindness in his voice which told Alice more than any string of words could. A simple 'thank-you' was all he needed to say.

'Just don't go getting yourself kidnapped, you twit!' She playfully slapped him on the chest, and Sam's mood seemed to brighten a bit.

'Easier said than done, apparently,' he replied with a wry smile.

'Would you-?' They both began to say in unison, but cut each other off mid-sentence. After a brief moment of almost painful politeness, insisting to one another that the other should finish their sentence first, Sam eventually relented.

'I, uh, was going to ask… Would you mind if I stay here? Just for a little while. It's just that with Men in Black abducting me from my place in the middle of the night, it's probably not wise if I go straight back home. I'm in no rush to repeat this whole ordeal again any time soon, and it'll be safer if I lay low for a bit. I can just crash on your sofa.

If you don't mind, of course? I'll be no trouble at all!'

This last part was not entirely true. Although it couldn't be said that Sam Hain himself was trouble - he certainly tried his best not to be - it was more the fact that trouble always seemed to inexorably follow him wherever he went.

'Of course,' Alice said. She felt relieved by his request. 'Actually, I was going to ask you if you wanted to stay here too. I thought you might not feel safe being back there yet after what happened... And to be honest, after tonight, I don't really want to be on my own.' She looked at Sam sheepishly. She had never been very good at admitting when she felt vulnerable, but tonight was an exception and all Alice wanted was a sense of security.

He nodded understandingly. 'Yeah, me neither.'

While Alice continued to rummage for her keys, eventually producing them triumphantly and unlocking the door to the building, Sam was saying his goodbyes to James. 'Honestly, I can't thank you enough. What you lot put yourselves through to get me out was nothing short of incredible. And... I'm sorry, about Cypher. If I hadn't been in that stupid mess, none of this would've happened.'

'Hey, when a shadowy secret society is out to get you, there's only so much you can blame yourself for,' James said, managing a smile, 'besides, I'm the one who got Cypher involved.

His sacrifice wasn't in vain, though. I'm going to have to keep telling myself that one, too.'

Bidding a final goodbye, James slowly pulled away from the front of the Islington townhouse. Filled with gratitude, Sam watched the car drive off down the road and around the corner, disappearing into the night. He turned and walked back towards the house, where Alice was stood waiting for him in the open doorway.

'Mind if I put the kettle on?' Sam asked as he stepped over the threshold and started to follow Alice up the stairs to her flat. 'It's been over twenty-four hours since I last had a cup of tea. The Regents have no idea how to treat guests.'

EPILOGUE

Rachel woke up the following morning to the incessant and irritating beeping of her alarm. She dozily tapped her phone and dropped it onto the pillow next to her, wrapping her duvet around herself and curling up into a ball. Five minutes later, her phone started beeping again, and with a moan of frustration she rolled out of bed. She sleepily swayed as she made her way out of her bedroom, and caught sight of herself in the mirror, her half-awake face gazing back at her and framed by a mess of long brunette hair. Mornings were not for her.

The crisp light of dawn was creeping in through the living room window, casting dust-mote filled beams into the room, but she barely even noticed how nice the morning was as she trudged into the kitchen. She filled the kettle with water and flicked the switch down. Rachel habitually adjusted the waistband of her thong and lazily scratched her buttocks. With a loud and luxuriating yawn, she raised her arms high above her head and stretched herself out as much as she could, causing her t-shirt to ride up above her navel. She concluded she couldn't really be bothered with making a proper breakfast this morning, and instead pulled a packet of pain au chocolat out of the cupboard.

The kettle began to hiss and occasionally made a banging sound, as if to reassure her that it was putting some real effort into boiling. Operating on autopilot, she tipped a spoonful of coffee granules into a mug and poured the boiling water in immediately after. She shoved one of the sweet rolls into her mouth, flakes of pastry scattering down the front of her t-shirt, and with coffee in hand she started back towards the living room.

She picked up the remote and flicked the TV on. A news report was detailing what was suspected to have been a gas explosion in the area of Regent's Park, which had disturbed a number of local residents in the small hours of the morning. The situation, the news reporter assured viewers, was under control and had not caused any harm or property damage.

It was only then that something startled her into wakefulness.

A low, guttural noise, somewhere between a moan and a growl, rumbled from somewhere in the room. Rachel froze, and she was sure her heart had skipped a beat. She was suddenly on edge, her heart pounding heavily in her chest, and she cast a wary but still sleep-blurred eye around the room. She turned around. There, on the sofa, was a shapeless black mass, heaving and shifting unnaturally. The form jolted suddenly with another groan, and a very human foot emerged from one end of it. She began to back away from it slowly, and as Rachel's eyes began to focus on the shapeless form she started to make sense of it. It wasn't shapeless at all; it was a man, his feet hanging off of one end of the sofa and his head - a mass of unruly dark hair - hanging off of the other. A large black greatcoat was draped over him like a blanket, and a fedora hat lay forlornly on the floor by the side of him.

Rachel very quickly abandoned her coffee and breakfast. Pulling her t-shirt down as far as possible, barely covering her thong and buttocks, she scuttered out of the living room as fast as she could and into Alice's room. She shook her friend gently, and then a little more forcefully, awake.

Alice, who was no more dressed and far less awake than her flatmate, stared up at her with bleary eyes. 'Wuh?' She managed to utter, her voice quiet and croaky.

'Why is there a strange man on the sofa?' Rachel asked, almost accusingly.

'Huh? Oh, he's... He's not that strange when you get to know him, really.' Alice rolled over and snuggled back into her pillow, asleep.

About the Author

Bron James is an author of science fiction, fantasy and magical realism. He was born with a silver pen in his mouth and has been making up stories for as long as he can remember. His professional début work of fiction, the first instalment of the *Sam Hain* series of novellas, was first published in 2013.

Born and raised in the south of England, Bron presently lives in London where he writes stories, drinks tea, and dreams improbable dreams.

~

www.bronjames.co.uk

MORE TITLES IN THE *SAM HAIN* SERIES

~

www.samhainscasebook.co.uk